The Art of NAPPING AT WORK

The Art of
NAPPING
AT WORK

*The no-cost, natural way to increase
productivity and satisfaction*

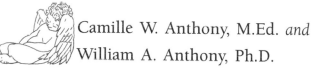 Camille W. Anthony, M.Ed. *and*
William A. Anthony, Ph.D.

On the cover: *La Méridienne,* by Vincent Van Gogh (1853–1890), by
permission of Musée d'Orsay, Paris © Photo RMN-Hervé Lewandowski

International Standard Book Number: 0-943914-95-7
Library of Congress Catalog Card Number: 99-73731

Published for The Napping Company, Inc. by
Larson Publications
a division of the Paul Brunton Philosophic Foundation
4936 NYS Route 414, Burdett, New York 14818 USA

05 04 03 02 01 00 99

10 9 8 7 6 5 4 3 2

CONTENTS

ACKNOWLEDGMENTS

WE acknowledge the following individuals and companies whose promotion of workplace napping continued to encourage us throughout the writing of this book.

Shauna LaFauci; Priscilla Noyes; Katrina Resevic; Steve White; Chris Babowal, Babowal Associates; Priscilla Dwyer, Carpe Diem; Alan Lindsey, Burlington Northern Santa Fe Railway; Ed Colburn and Steve Mardon, Circadian Technologies; David Birch, Cognetics; Sandy Francis and Susie Campolong, Deloitte Consulting; Karen Gould, Gould Evans Goodman; Dorothy Granger, Granger Financial Services; Russ Klettke, Klettke Associates; Mary Ann Whitlock, Microtek; Kimberly Oliver, OP Contract; Wayne Papowich, Siecor; Maggie Forbes, Sprint; Stewart Ugelow and Eric Ng, Student.Net; Dennis Holland, Union Pacific Railroad; Regina Villa, Regina Villa Associates; Craig Yarde and Adam Glogowski, Yarde Metals.

"Right now employees are hiding their naps from their colleagues who are hiding their naps from them. And their bosses and supervisors are too tired to notice."

WORKPLACE NAPPING— AN IDEA WHOSE TIME HAS COME

A bedtime story

Once upon a time two nervous parents named Camille and Bill took their sick daughter to a medical center for treatment. It was evening. They waited expectantly for the doctor who was "on call" to arrive. The nurse, with awe in her voice, told the apprehensive parents that the doctor had been extremely busy and hadn't slept or even napped in the last twenty hours. Bill was about to remark reverently about his deep gratitude for the doctor's martyr-like commitment to his patients. But before Bill could utter his fawning comments, Camille irreverently responded, "Well in that case find another doctor to see my sick child. I want a doctor who is awake and alert."

And so the story goes, and goes, and goes. In health care centers, in offices, on construction sites, in manufacturing settings, etc., sleeplessness is often perceived as a badge of honor—suggesting an ambitious and committed worker. Little thought seems to be given to the productivity, safety, and competitiveness of the sleep-deprived worker. The malady of sleep deprivation is often talked about with pride; its obvious solution—more sleep—is often talked about with dismay.

However, the survey says . . .

While workplace napping isn't talked about in public, we know it is practiced in private. One way we know this is from workers from all over the world who have completed our Workplace Napping Survey—the first and only one of its kind.

The Workplace Napping Survey is part of a larger ethnographic study (Gosh that sounds impressive!) we've been conducting on workplace napping. We have also interviewed countless workplace nappers, observed people napping, and read numerous accounts of napping at the workplace. As a sacrifice to science, we even have participated in the practice ourselves! We have also discussed the idea with bosses and supervisors and have recorded case histories of places of employment that support workplace napping. What we have learned will open the sleepy eyes of workers and bosses, and at some point—during a break from work—put you, the reader, to sleep!

Is that AN or PN?

This first chapter gives an overview of what's coming in the book. Each following chapter should be read in one sitting—or sleeping. The best time to read a chapter is either after a nap or prior to a nap.

Actually, prior to a nap and after a nap are the two major parts of a workday. PN (prior to the nap) and AN (after the nap) may replace AM and PM as the proper way to divide a workday. The operative question becomes, "Was that PN or AN?"—as in the sentence: "Did you read the first chapter before or after your nap?" Example of an answer: "It was a PN read, during my lunch break."

After reading this overview, use your own judgment about the best time to read another chapter. And remember, there are really only two times during a workday that matter: AN and PN!

Is anybody out there awake?

Since the invention of the light bulb, people are sleeping one to two hours less each night. There is so much more to do after dark now than at the last turn of a century. We can work at night and play at night. And many of us choose to "do it all" —except sleep! We don't envision our culture reverting back to 19th-century nighttime sleep patterns. For the foreseeable future, the workplace will be populated by sleepy workers whose productivity, safety, health, concentration, and mood are adversely affected by lack of sleep. Unless . . .

Sleep researchers who study napping behavior (whose science we whimsically call nonapapology!) report that most people who live in non-siesta cultures are sleep deprived. We're not talking here about people with sleep disorders. We're talking about the populace at large. However, rather than pejoratively describe all these people as sleep deprived, we prefer to call them nap-ready.

Are you kidding me?

Not surprisingly, most of the workers who adamantly resist the idea of workplace napping are bosses and supervisors. Allowing a sleepy worker to sleep (it seems so obvious a solution to us) is seen as rewarding for a slothful lifestyle and/or a shoddy work ethic. Worker productivity and worker napping are viewed as at opposite ends of the spectrum, i. e., one can't be both a good worker and a good workplace napper.

Yet these same bosses and supervisors do provide breaks from work. There are lunch breaks, coffee breaks, and smoke breaks, but no such thing as a nap break. The other types of breaks are sanctioned as helping workers to be more satisfied and productive. Unfortunately, if a worker wishes to

THE ART OF NAPPING AT WORK

nap at the workplace, even while on one of those sanctioned breaks, they must "sneak" a nap, "steal" a nap, or worry about getting "caught napping" (when there really is no crime to catch).

Workplace napping is as simple as counting sheep

The thesis of this book is simple. Sleepiness is rampant and is affecting worker productivity and satisfaction. Too many workers are tired. Allowing them to nap during their breaks can increase their productivity and their mood. Workplace napping makes both economic sense and common sense.

While the organization may own the workplace, managers in a fully functioning organization know they don't own the worker. We think that some organizations' poor attitudes about workplace napping are due to their belief that workplace nappers want to nap *on* the job rather than *at* the job. The difference between *on* and *at* is a major distinction that can make or break an organization's attitudes toward workplace napping.

A workplace epidemic

The realization of the benefits of workplace napping must come soon, because an epidemic is affecting more than 50 percent of American adults. Non-siesta cultures around the world are similarly afflicted. The epidemic is called sleep deprivation and its most obvious signs appear in our working life. Sleep-deprived workers are less productive and more prone to accidents.

As a matter of fact, because of auto accidents caused by sleepy drivers, workers are less likely even to get to work! Sleepiness is right behind drunkenness as the primary cause of auto accidents. Each year 250,000 auto accidents and 10,000 fatalities are due to falling asleep at the wheel, according to the Highway Safety Commission.

Industrial accidents increase at—guess when?—the preferred workplace napping time, between 1 and 4 P.M. The Better Sleep Council reported that a third of their respondents to a survey said that lack of sleep was affecting job performance.

Like most epidemics, sleep deprivation is caused by a virus running rampant. Its medical name is the "sleepy-dust virus" and its mode of transmission is well known. Sleepy-dust virus is communicated not through the air or by contact, but by our culture.

Is there a cure for this epidemic?

Fortunately, the cure exists. This major workplace problem has an easy solution—one that is natural and free.

Workplace napping can both prevent and cure the effects of sleepy-dust virus. Workplace napping is one of a few habits that's good for you (improves your mood), good for your employer (improves your productivity), good for your personal relationships (makes you more attentive), and good for your country (decreases accidents). Workplace napping is a concept that truly rivals motherhood and apple pie!

While for many of us workplace napping is an idea whose time has come, implementing such a healthy activity will be difficult.

Responses to our Workplace Napping Survey clearly indicate why the practice remains secret. Survey respondents mince no words when they say why they don't nap publicly at work. Covert workplace nappers feel that overt napping would put their job at risk. "I would be fired, no questions asked," is but one example of how workers express this concern.

Our culture erects impediments to the cure for sleep deprivation but not to the spread of the epidemic. These cultural barriers are both attitudinal and environmental.

Changing the workplace culture

Like so many other good ideas that directly oppose our prevailing culture, workplace napping is not an easy sell. (Neither, for that matter, was fluoride in the drinking water or women wearing slacks to work.) Even when the evidence of health problems associated with smoking became well known, prohibiting workplace smoking took a while. Endorsing workplace napping will also take an organized campaign targeting one industry at a time. It won't happen in forty winks!

Like stopping workplace smoking, starting workplace napping is a habit change that's healthy. Sleepy-dust can replace smoke as the foreign object to eliminate in the workplace atmosphere.

As exemplified by workplace smoking behavior, the workplace culture can be changed. But permitting and even encouraging workplace napping will be an equally traumatic change for many employers. Are employers ready to hear that Mary took a work break and was napping before her major presentation to the board, or that John is going to have a nap-break before he finishes his report? Will such information generate confidence or concern in the boss—or in one's fellow employees? All types of people on the organizational chart have to realize the many advantages of workplace napping. By instituting the practice of "productivity" napping, one can in actuality sleep oneself up the corporate ladder.

Attitudinal barriers

As our survey shows, anyone who has attempted or even thought of taking a public nap in the workplace knows about attitudinal barriers to workplace napping. Workers tell us repeatedly that they would feel guilty or ashamed, or worse, get fired, if they were ever "caught napping" at work.

Nappers are a creative group, and they have devised many innovative ways to get around attitudinal barriers as well as environmental barriers. One woman told us that attitudinal barriers have prompted her to nap in the restroom. She closes the door to the stall, sits on the toilet fully clothed, and naps. When she awakens she leaves—but not without first flushing! Perhaps as attitudinal barriers to workplace napping begin to crumble she will at least be able to nap without flushing.

Architectural barriers

Poor attitudes towards workplace napping (or napping anywhere) have also erected architectural barriers to workplace napping. We hear many reports of bosses and supervisors who deliberately buy furniture that makes napping difficult.

Years ago, manufacturers tried to speed up the assembly line to improve productivity. It didn't work. In a similar fashion, some employers have stripped down the workplace environment to discourage napping. It won't work either. Hard, straight-backed lounge chairs, the absence of couches, overly bright lights, etc., won't make tired workers more productive. It will make them more tired and more disgruntled.

Speeding up the assembly line and stripping down the workplace environment are comparable in their misguided efforts to increase worker performance. There are physical limits to workplace labor. Environments in tune with these limits can increase worker performance.

What message is sent to employees when their employers purposely inhibit workplace napping? And what message is sent when the company facilitates workplace napping by making the environment nap friendly?

Many bosses think that the former sends the message that work is expected to be hard—as hard as the furniture. In contrast, the latter may say that we care about your health and your work. For what it's worth, we've heard from many employers that a more satisfied worker leads to a more satisfied customer.

Favorite workplace napping places

In spite of the difficult workplace environment for napping, many people do nap at work. Only some nap openly; most must nap in secret. Many speak passionately about their favorite workplace napping spot.

The ingenuity of workplace nappers is unmatched. In their chairs, on their desks, under their desks (like George in a classic Seinfeld episode), in their cars, in the bathroom, on a bench, in the cockpit (we're not exaggerating here), in closets, on the floor, in the lounge, just about anywhere you might imagine, workers have tried napping. Just like the song that says, "everybody has to have a laughing place," so "every workplace napper has to have a napping place." Whether it's public or private, soft or hard, workers come up with their own favorite spot. Like Goldilocks, they look and look until they find the place that's "just right."

Because workplace nappers usually must nap secretly, many of them don't realize that their favorite napping place is also someone else's favorite napping place. For example, people who nap in their cars in the company parking lot (or perhaps several miles off the company's premises) typically think that they are the only ones who nap in their cars. Yet carnapping (not to be confused with stealing a car) is a preferred workplace nap option, albeit one kept secret from one's colleagues, some of whom are also napping in the same lot.

Doing it well

Once you have discovered some favorite napping places, then you want to make sure you get the most out of your naps. There isn't one napping style. Nappers are unique people, and their uniqueness carries over to their napping behavior. Nappers don't worry about "doing it right," but they do wish to do it well

Some nappers wonder how to avoid long periods of grogginess after they awake; others want to learn how to wake up after a certain nap length; others wish to fall asleep sooner. Every napper is a potential source of learning for another napper, but there are general points one can make about napping well. Borrowing unashamedly from Steven Covey's enormously successful concept, these points have come to be known in the napping community as *Seven Habits of Highly Effective Workplace Nappers*:

1. *Announce your nap to yourself and if possible to your colleagues.*

2. *Gather your napnomic devices (things that help you nap).*

3. *Ensure a method for on-time awakening.*

4. *Ensure control of your nap environment, including a plan to avoid* nappus interruptus.

5. *Revel in the nap.*

6. *Deal with sleep inertia, if necessary.*

7. *Begin to plan your next nap as you awaken from this nap.*

A policy on napping

Some workplace napping policies are implicit. That is, neither the boss nor the supervisors have ever said anything about napping to the employees who nap publicly. But even in these organizations, some workplace nappers may feel uncomfortable when the policy is only implicit.

In other workplaces a favorable napping policy is explicit, and nappers perform at their best—both in their work and in their napping. There may be a special room or place set aside for napping (i.e., a napnasium), or the boss or supervisor may speak openly about the benefits of napping at work. In the latter instance, workers will find their own spot to nap—with no special architectural changes needed from the employer.

Camille's previous boss, Regina Villa of Regina Villa Associates, has been explicit about the benefits of workplace napping for those who choose to do it. She realizes that a nap and productivity go hand in hand and has allowed any employees who wish to do so to take that much needed nap. If she happened to call Camille at work when Camille was napping she would typically have Camille call her back after Camille woke up. Bosses this enlightened about the benefits of workplace napping, both to the company and to its employees, are far too rare!

But the trend for workplace napping has begun, and now more workplace nappers and their bosses are ready to lie down and be counted! In 1998, *Kiplinger* magazine's annual forecast issue spoke of napping as an up-and-coming method to help employees become more productive. In the 21st century, workplace napping will be an accepted, productivity-enhancing company benefit, rather than secretive company practice.

Telenapping

There are millions of people who *are* already napping openly at work—but few of their colleagues see them. These expert nappers are telecommuting—and telenapping. Napping at the home workplace is, in fact, one reason why telecommuting is becoming so popular. Working only steps from one's bed or couch is one of the great worker benefits of all time!

The number of workers telecommuting is growing dramatically. Ask them about the advantages of working at home. If they are reluctant to mention napping as a benefit, ask directly about it—and watch a satisfied smile sweep across their face. Telenapping workers have the best of both worlds—the world of being awake and the world of being asleep. They can be more productive in both worlds.

Napping while *you work*

Napping *at* work is coming. Will napping *while* working be far behind? More and more employers are awakening, albeit slowly, to the benefits of workplace napping. The next napping breakthrough will come when employers recognize that people can nap *and* work at the same time. Airplane pilots are a great example of workplace napping, although most passengers who don't believe in the productivity of napping would not wish to think about their pilot napping during the flight.

Historical figures napped while working. Brahms napped at the piano while he composed the music for what has come to be known as Brahms' Lullaby. No wonder it's such great napping music. Napoleon napped during his battles. Is that a part of the Napoleonic complex? The organic structure of benzene (one of the great scientific achievements of the 19th century) was discovered while the discoverer was napping! Already the query, "Have you tried sleeping on it?" is a part of our lexicon. In the not too distant future, employers will ask their employees, "Have you tried napping on it?"

"Napping while you work" will replace "whistling while you work" as the hallmark of a satisfied, productive worker. And maybe in the not too distant future there will be three parts to a workday PN, AN, & DN—as in During the Nap.

z   z   z

Napping and productivity go hand in hand, see eye to eye, fit hand in glove, and lie side by side.

NAPPING AND
A PRODUCTIVE WORK FORCE

Workplace napping and common sense

Nap researchers (nonapapologists) have learned scientifically what nappers have learned experientially. Napping is good for you. It improves mood and performance. One can be a more productive worker *and* a workplace napper.

Napping does make sense to Chris Babowal, CEO of Babowal Associates. The company provides educational and testing services worldwide and has reaped the rewards of a nap-friendly policy for their instructors. The mandatory "recuperative break" between classes gives employees a napping opportunity and has resulted in livelier, more interesting instruction, happier clients, and increased contracts for the training company.

Unlike Chris Babowal, some workers and some employers are simply not going to believe that napping at the workplace can improve worker productivity. They need objective, scientific studies to support this thesis. So let's go to the data.

Sleep statistics and sleepiness

But first a word of caution: In preparing this book, we reviewed numerous studies and written material on sleepiness and productivity. Well-written, well-conceived, and highly informative as they were, as a group these reports drove us to nap. They told us what our workplace napping surveys told us, but without the personal flavor and napping anecdotes (napidotes) we get in the Workplace Napping Survey and our interviews with workplace nappers.

Nevertheless, some employers and employees want to be convinced with percentages and controlled laboratory studies. For the next several pages only, we'll give some facts about sleeping and productivity—facts that reinforce what our mothers told us years ago: "Get some sleep and you'll feel better and do better."

Many people believe statistics don't lie, only statisticians do. We tend to agree, but for different reasons. We believe statistics don't lie either—they make you fall asleep before you get a chance to hear any lies! But when some statistics are repeated over and over, people do tend to believe them.

And that is what we find when we read the literature written by nona-papologists. Over and over again we hear that the majority (slightly over 50%) of American adults are sleep deprived. This statistic has led *us* to conclude that these adults are in reality "nap-ready." A final word of caution: Don't read these next several pages if you are about to drive or operate heavy machinery!

Sleep deprivation and its consequences

- A Harris Poll concluded that nearly half of the American work force say they have experienced episodes of sleeplessness in recent months; two-thirds of these workers say that sleeplessness negatively affects their work performance. In particular, they report that feeling sleepy adversely impacts their concentration, decision-making, problem-solving, handling of stressful situations, listening to others, and relating to co-workers.

- A Gallup poll found that even among adults who report getting as much sleep as they need, three quarters of these supposedly well-rested adults experience daytime sleepiness. A large majority agree that feeling tired or sleepy during the day can have a negative effect on one's productivity.

- Examining the impact of sleep deprived workers from a different perspective, it has been estimated that sleepy people are responsible for

60–90% of all industrial accidents. The Exxon Valdez and Chernobyl are among the most notable and expensive examples.

- Sleepy people are also responsible for accidents getting to and from work. The United States National Highway Traffic Safety Administration reported that 25% of recently surveyed drivers admitted to falling asleep while driving, and one in twenty reported having had an accident due to sleepiness while driving

- The New York Thruway has estimated that about one-third of their fatal crashes are caused by drowsy drivers. The AAA Foundation–sponsored Drive Alert/Arrive Alert Campaign is just what we nappers have ordered.

Sleep cents

So what is the economic cost of sleep deprivation and lost productivity? It's huge enough to get your attention. How huge depends, as you might expect, on who's doing the figuring. Here are some of the numbers.

- According to a 1997 survey commissioned by the National Sleep Foundation, sleep loss costs U.S. employers approximately 18 billion dollars a year in lost productivity

- The National Highway Traffic Safety Administration estimates that crashes due to driver fatigue cause Americans 12.5 billion dollars per year in reduced productivity and property loss.

- Congress has entered into the statistics game as well. A congressional resolution estimates the cost to American families and businesses of sleep problems as 100 billion dollars per year in lost productivity and opportunity.

No matter what estimates you use, sleepy people are causing significant damage to the economy and to themselves. If you combine the effects of sleep deprivation due to lost productivity, lost wages, lost lives, and lost mental function, you are talking about a major work-force problem. And these losses don't even take into account other aspects of daily living, such as overall health, relationships with family and friends, one's ability to pursue personal interests, etc. Surveys indicate that the majority of employed adults feel sleeplessness affects them in each of these areas as well. We have yet to hear of a company that is not searching for ways to improve the bottom line, the quarterly report, or the earnings per share. It's time to wake up to all of the many negative effects of sleep deprivation.

Getting more and better nighttime sleep

You might say that sleep deprivation and its effect on productivity and costs could be solved easily if people could just sleep better at night. A work force that sleeps long and well at night would certainly be the ideal. But to expect most workers to be sufficiently rested by their nighttime sleep, you'd have to be dreaming!

Americans now average six hours, fifty-seven minutes of sleep a night—

significantly less then they report they need, and less than the eight hours many people hold up as the gold standard of nighttime sleep. Our average nighttime sleep is *way* less than the nearly ten hours of nighttime sleep we had before Edison invented the light bulb.

The reason a daytime nap is an obvious solution to sleep deprivation is because our culture seems unwilling to adapt to more nighttime sleep. Two-income families, late-night television, a long commute, shift work, organized kids' activities, and the like are deeply ingrained. Our busy home life and work life conspire together to reduce our nighttime sleep.

Besides those of us who know we are sleep deprived, many individuals who think they are doing "just fine" on the sleep they get, are in actuality sleep deprived and don't even know it! A very telling study on people who believed they were well rested found that 30% revealed sleep deprivation when given a sleep latency test. Many macho-types who say they can function well on very little sleep don't really know what it's like to be awake and alert. After a beneficial change in their sleep patterns, they may find themselves truly conscious for the first time in a long time.

Napping is normal

Science is at the napper's bedside. Nonapapologists believe that we may actually be "biphasic," in that our activity patterns are naturally separated by two periods of sleep—nocturnal and mid-afternoon. Our capacity to nap during the day is biological, and due to our circadian rhythms. About mid-way between waking up and bed time, our body goes through physiological changes—including changes in body temperature and alertness. The drop in body temperature and alertness which we experience at night during sleep is mirrored by a similar but smaller drop in the middle of the day.

The Encyclopedia of Sleep and Dreaming states: "There is a biologically based tendency to fall asleep in mid-afternoon just as there is a tendency to fall asleep at night. Moreover if sleep the night before is reduced or disturbed for any reason, a nap the subsequent afternoon is not only more likely to occur, but it also can relieve sleepiness and enhance alertness."

Napping is natural, not only for humans but also for many animals. Don't visit a zoo in the mid-afternoon because you'll see mostly sleepy, napping animals. You certainly won't see animals performing. If you visit the corporate zoo during mid-afternoon you might also notice a dip in performance, albeit more subtle. Like their mammalian counterparts, corporate performers won't be engaging in antics at the monkey bars; rather, their most productive performance will be at the coffee bar.

The predisposition to nap in the mid-afternoon—which many of us think is primarily due to eating lunch, attending boring meetings, and/or doing repetitive tasks—is in actuality a function of our biology. The activities that we believe cause the nap actually just unmask the physiological tendency to nap which is already there.

Some findings from nonapapology

The findings of nonapapology have been available for several decades. But like many scientific findings, it is taking a long time for the discoveries to be put into practice. As early as the 1970s nonapapologists reported performance improvements in non-sleep-deprived, healthy young adults during the hour after a nap. These naps occurred in the morning, afternoon, or evening and varied in duration from a half-hour to two hours.

Performance enhancement after daytime napping in non-sleep-deprived adults has also been found many hours after the nap period (from $1\frac{1}{2} - 10$ hours later). We call these naps "preparatory naps," as they prepare one to perform for longer periods of wakefulness after the nap is over. Preparatory naps are helpful when adults are going to enter a period of prolonged wakefulness (e.g., long work hours). When sleep deprivation is already present (e.g., during a long period of extensive work activity), napping can prevent some of the performance deterioration that typically results.

An added piece of good news: In healthy adults, napping does not affect nocturnal sleep. A good daytime nap *and* a good nighttime sleep—who could ask for anything more?

Nonapapology around the world

In a U.S. Army study, the effects of preparatory naps on mood, alertness, and performance were compared to a forced rest period. Following the naps or rest period subjects remained awake for 23 additional hours. Compared to a forced rest break with no sleep, the nap break yielded better results.

In a Swedish study of napping and daytime alertness, researchers measured the alertness of the same eight men on three different occasions: after a full night's sleep, after four hours of sleep and a short nap, and after four hours of sleep with no nap. A full night's sleep yielded the highest level of alertness, and the no-nap condition yielded the lowest level of alertness. Not surprisingly (at least to us), the folks who had four hours of sleep plus a short nap performed as well on a computer alertness task as they did after a full night's sleep.

Nonapapologists in Japan studied the effects of a 20-minute nap after lunch. The subjects participated in napping and no-napping conditions at intervals of one week. For the nap condition, subjects started at 12:20 P.M. and were awakened after they had slept 20 minutes. The nap improved self-ratings of sleepiness and task performance.

Napping is being studied around the world. It's time for workers and bosses "to wake up and smell the coffee" when it comes to the benefits of workplace napping.

And speaking of coffee

While afternoon naps are increasingly popular, they're still not commonly talked about or practiced openly except in sleep research studies. Subjects in one research study reported that their naps most often occur mid-way between when they wake up in the morning and go to sleep at night—or, said another way, during the afternoon coffee break time!

Coffee has been our typical response to sleep deprivation, but coffee doesn't preclude napping as well. A series of English studies have examined the effects of caffeine and napping on performance in a car simulator. The research has shown that either caffeine or a brief nap can effectively reduce sleepiness in drivers for one hour.

These researchers also examined coffee and napping combined, taken during a 30-minute driving break, prior to a two-hour continuous, monotonous afternoon drive in a car simulator. The combined treatment of napping plus coffee reduced the driver "incidents" significantly versus the caffeine condition alone. Coffee after a nap seems to be an acceptable way to overcome the performance decrements brought about by sleepiness.

We aren't necessarily recommending that a nap break replace the mid-afternoon coffee break. For coffee aficionados, it doesn't have to be one or the other. Both help combat the mid-afternoon dip in performance and mood. (Though unfortunately, coffee alone is often the only acceptable option.)

Coffee lovers can be nap lovers also. There is a need for both, albeit one need is biological and the other learned. Coffee and cream, coffee and sugar, coffee and napping: all appealing combinations at the workplace!

THE ART OF NAPPING AT WORK

Enough of this laboratory data

Stop already—this research is making my eyes glaze over! More and more data will only confirm the obvious:

> *Workers are sleep deprived,*
>
> *Sleep deprivation negatively affects mood and performance,*
>
> *Napping is a normal response to sleep deprivation (and life in general); and*
>
> *Napping improves both mood and performance.*

Nonapaplogists around the world have lauded the positive, life-enhancing effects of napping. The workplace epidemic of sleepy-dust virus (Latin: *somnolentus dustus*) has prevented too many workers and bosses from seeing the facts.

On a positive note, sleep researchers have apparently convinced the U.S. judicial system that sleepiness is rampant in the American workplace. A recent ruling by the U.S. Circuit Court of Appeals gave another trial to a defendant who argued that his attorney was napping for most of the trial! The judges stated, "There are states of drowsiness that come over everyone from time to time during a working day." Thank you, your honor, for upholding the obvious—at least to those of us who admit to being workplace nappers.

And someone please tell that lawyer to read *The Art of Napping*—our general treatise on napping and the pioneer companion of this book—for important tips on nap management strategies!

People are talking about workplace napping

Just as important as laboratory data is what people are saying about workplace napping. Workers who won't nap openly at the workplace do talk openly about it to us. We ask about it at parties, on airplanes, and at business meetings. Everybody has an opinion and wants to express it. Intrigued and unbowed, we posted The Workplace Napping Survey online at www.napping.com.

Some facts about the Workplace Napping Survey

The Workplace Napping Survey has been publicized in media outlets as varied as *The Financial Times of London, Self* magazine, the *Boston Globe,* the BBC, and various business newsletters. As can be seen in our survey, we're particularly interested in certain aspects of workplace napping. We want to know the occupations, age, and gender of workplace nappers. If people take the time to fill out the survey but are not workplace nappers, we want to know why not.

For people who admit to napping at work (a healthy majority—in more ways than one—of those who have so far filled out the survey online), we want to know if they nap publicly or secretly. We want to know some details about their napping activity: where they nap, when and for how long; are they groggy after waking up and for how long? And how do they avoid being disturbed by others?

And more

We also want to know if they use workplace napnomic devices. Napnomic devices are things that help you to nap, such as a mat, a pillow, or blanket. (Early napnomic devices are a teddy bear, pacifier, crib blanket, bottle, etc). Furthermore, we want to know why they nap and what their colleagues think about their workplace napping.

For workplace nappers and non-nappers alike, we solicit examples of how sleepiness on the job may cause poor performance or accidents. From both groups we also want to know about the workplace napping environment. For example, is there an explicit or implicit napping policy at work? How comfortable would they be approaching their employer to talk about the nap policy? Do they have any idea how many of their colleagues nap at the workplace?

As enthusiastic ethnographers we ourselves participate in the activity under study as often as we can. We survey people from all walks of life. In groups and individually we interview workers and their bosses. We do case histories of companies that presently allow workplace napping. Finally, we observe people openly napping at work.

We're having a marvelous adventure collecting this data. We hope you have as much enjoyment reading about workplace napping and its glorious possibilities. What follows are pieces of information, stories, and ideas for those who enjoy workplace napping now and for all those who have thought about workplace napping—that is, a majority of the work force!

z   z   z

The lack of a soft couch at work is not the major barrier. It's our colleagues' hardened attitudes.

Overcoming Attitudinal Barriers

"I'm Tom and I'm a workplace napper"

To healthy applause and appreciative laughter, Tom, an earnest and tweedy looking man in his mid-thirties, courageously announced his workplace napping to 200 colleagues at a conference entitled "Working ourselves to death." With that brief self-deprecating statement, Tom simultaneously broke free of the malevolent attitudes others had of his behavior and poked fun at how society perceives workplace napping.

Many workplace nappers, unlike Tom, believe they need to be secretive and ashamed. Many who speak to us wish to remain anonymous. This chapter focuses on how attitudes about napping at the workplace force this normal, natural way to increasing worker productivity under the covers.

Nappism at the workplace

"Nappism" is the napping vocabulary word we coined to describe society's prejudicial attitudes toward napping. Napping stigma spreads into the workplace from the culture at large. Historically, napping was sometimes thought to be a disorder, a reflection of abnormality. Others said that a propensity to take naps indicates "poor sleep hygiene." (We aren't sure exactly what that means, and we won't ask!)

Our impression is that nappism is due to the fact that napping is a behavior openly practiced by the very young and very old. Infants and seniors are the age groups with the greatest opportunity to nap with impunity. The prejudice toward napping as a non-productive behavior illustrates our general intolerance for the contribution these age groups make to society. If an otherwise healthy working-age adult naps in public, she or he is considered lazy or slothful.

What to say if "caught" napping at work

We, of course, don't believe you owe any defensive explanation with respect to napping at work. However, we've been sent variations of this list of

explanations numerous times, and the fact that it is whimsical makes it worth repeating. If you're of the playful nature, try one of these statements. If you're of the playful and proselytizing nature, say one of these statements and give the other person *The Art of Napping at Work* to read themselves to sleep!

"They told me at the blood bank this might happen."

"This is just a 15-minute power-nap, like they raved about in the management courses I'm taking at night and on weekends."

"Whew! Guess I left the top off the liquid paper."

"I wasn't sleeping! I was meditating on the mission statement and envisioning a new paradigm!"

"This is one of the seven habits of highly effective people."

"I was testing the keyboard for drool resistance."

"Actually, I'm doing a "Stress Level Elimination Exercise Plan" (SLEEP). I learned it at the last mandatory seminar you made me attend."

"I was doing a highly specific yoga exercise to relieve work related stress."

"Darn! Why did you interrupt me? I had almost figured out a solution to our biggest problem."

"The coffee machine is broken . . ."

"Someone must have put decaf in the wrong pot."

"Boy, that cold medicine I took last night just won't wear off!"

"Ah, the unique and unpredictable circadian rhythms of the workaholic!"

"I wasn't sleeping, I was trying to pick up my contact lens without using my germ-laden hands."

"Amen."

Non-nappers' attitudes

Some respondents to the Workplace Napping Survey are non-nappers. Even though they don't nap at work, they take the time to tell us why they do not. The survey also asks if they are ever sleepy on the job, and if so what productivity problems this causes. Answers to why folks don't nap at the workplace can be divided into three categories with respect to the source of these negative attitudes:

- The organization itself, as characterized by its implicit or explicit policies about workplace napping.

- The negative attitudes of colleagues. If their attitude is thought to be against napping at the workplace, they can inhibit the napping of other workers.

- The attitudes of the prospective nappers themselves. Sometimes people who want to nap at work incorporate the pejorative attitudes of fellow workers or the organization. Unwittingly, these potential nappers speak against napping at work because they are expected to act this way. Eventually they "identify with the aggressor" and start to believe that this is how they actually feel about it.

Let's examine in more detail how attitudes in each of these three categories are expressed. It will give practicing nappers and potential nappers a review of what they are up against in their quest for improving their own productivity and that of their organization through workplace napping.

Organizational attitudes

We have talked to bosses and supervisors who strongly defend their organization against those who might like to nap at the workplace. "Not on my time they don't—if they want to sleep they can do that somewhere else." When we ask these staunch defenders of proper workplace behavior whether or not they let their workers use the bathroom, have a break from work, eat lunch, and drink coffee, they look at us as if we're "out of touch." And "out of touch" is exactly how we feel they are when they tell us their views on workplace napping. Unless workers are doing something immoral or illegal during their break time, we believe they should be able to do as they please. Napping would appear to meet the test of morality and legality.

Workplace nappers don't wish to offend or embarrass the organization. They just want to be productive, and napping can improve their productivity. Food, exercise, and sleep are the basic elements of productivity—and of life itself. All organizations countenance food and exercise during breaks. Why not sleep? Napping during the workday has to be seen as essential as food and movement during the workday.

The Survey says . . .

The comments of non-nappers are particularly telling when it comes to the attitudes of many organizations toward workplace napping. Many non-nappers who complete the Workplace Napping Survey seem to be *great* candidates for workplace napping. But, they say that the organization would not tolerate such behavior. Their comments ranged widely. For example:

- A 47-year-old, male production manager put it rather bluntly: "The bastards won't let me."

- Another non-napper, a female business manager, age 33, expressed her company's napping policies in a more subtle manner: "Our office doesn't seem to be accepting to napping."

For the most part, non-nappers who attribute their lack of napping behavior to organizational attitudes say they fear being fired from their job. Such fears are expressed in many different phrases. "I might lose my job if caught napping." "Sleeping on the job is grounds for dismissal." "I would be arrested." (military personnel) Some organizations have *explicit* policies that napping is prohibited anytime—including lunch or break time.

Still other non-nappers believe there is an implied message that while napping might not get you fired, it will certainly affect your reputation as a good worker.

- A 19-year-old female office assistant replied, "My supervisors would get mad if they caught me sleeping on the job. They would be like, 'you don't get paid to sleep here.'"

- A male economist, age 39, responded, "It would be frowned upon as loafing. Supervisors would feel very comfortable teasing nappers."

It appears that many supervisors are doing their organization's bidding (albeit causing low productivity) when they send the message that napping may cost your reputation, your job, or maybe both.

Colleagues' attitudes

Workers who don't nap at work also attribute their non-napping to the attitudes of fellow workers. They believe their co-workers would laugh at them, tease them, stigmatize them, turn them in, or in general just make them feel embarrassed. For example:

- A female bill collector, age 26, indicated that being seen napping by her co-workers "would be very, very embarrassing."

- Reporting from a company that we would not want to work for, a male computer programmer was "worried that I may get busted by other workers."

- Another non-napper, a 36-year-old male (no occupation given) expresses

THE ART OF NAPPING AT WORK

an interesting twist: "I'm intimidated by younger workers who seem to possess more energy . . . fear of being labeled as lazy." So rather than this worker being perceived as somebody who knows how to ensure his productivity by taking care of himself by napping, he fears being derogated by his own colleagues if seen napping at work.

Pejorative attitudes about workplace napping exist around the world The Workplace Napping Survey is available worldwide through the Internet, and some people take the time to indicate from what country they are responding.

- From France a 46-year-old salesman says that he doesn't nap at work because, "You will be judged as a real sloth by other workers."

- From the Netherlands a 29-year-old postmaster opined, "If colleagues see me, I will hang. There's no nap culture here in Holland. But it is well worth it to introduce because napping is not only good for productivity but it is also good for stress/unhappiness/depression/wrinkles."

We couldn't have said it better ourselves!

Worker attitudes

When workers internalize pernicious workplace attitudes toward napping, they inhibit their own ability to nap. These workers can't see themselves as one of those "evil nappers," so they never give themselves the opportunity to experience the joys of napping.

A 20-year-old female programmer wrote, "I don't feel right about it. I only nap if I fall asleep in my chair." We guess falling asleep in one's chair is somehow okay and different from napping!

Still other non-nappers suggest they have "never even thought about it." While this is hard to believe, we must agree that for some people (the minority) napping is just not a blip on their screen. As a matter of fact, in college Camille didn't even think about napping at school or at her part-time jobs.

Fortunately for her relationship with Bill, she was not a napaphobic (someone who tries to make nappers feel guilty or ashamed about napping). Bill napped regularly during their courtship and Camille never thought about joining in—or, more importantly, criticizing.

The minority who never nap and never even think about it must be tolerant of those who do. Napaphobia is a very real example of a minor-

THE ART OF NAPPING AT WORK

ity of people terrorizing the majority. Just as the attitudes of a minority of smokers once dominated the workplace, now it is a minority of non-nappers. Their days are truly numbered by the growing trend. Just as we do for smokers, maybe we will build special rooms for non-nappers—a spartanly furnished room where non-nappers can sit with other non-nappers and gaze somnolently at one another whenever they get sleepy at work. Their napping colleagues have no need for this "awake but asleep room" because they are out in the workplace napping as needed during their break—and then working with renewed vigor after their nap.

Non-nappers get sleepy at work too!

We weren't surprised that non-nappers exist, but we were surprised how readily they admit to becoming sleepy and non-productive at work. Even workers who don't nap because they've never thought about it or believe it wouldn't be right have thought about their lost productivity due to sleepiness. Non-nappers report three types of problems caused by sleepiness at work.

> *Sleepiness causes mental lapses (such as inability to concentrate)*
>
> *It causes physical problems (such as low energy levels)*
>
> *It causes emotional problems (such as inattentiveness to people)*

Non-nappers state that a variety of specific work tasks are affected by sleepiness at work: editing, filing, listening to customers, data entry, driving, reading, writing, scheduling, etc. Consider the following statements of non-nappers:

- A 29-year-old male quality engineer admitted to "filing information in the wrong place."

- A 22-year-old female administrative assistant wrote, "If I'm really tired, I'll schedule patients wrong for appointments."

- A production assistant, age 35, says that she does "a lot of reading and writing. My comprehensiveness and writing ability suffer in the early afternoon after lunch."

- A female corporate accountant, age 25, describes how her sleepiness affects everyone in the office: "People in my department notice my mood (I'm usually a pretty happy person—but only if I get sleep), and my sleepiness affects the tone of our department."

- And our personal favorite from a 28-year-old female corporate communications manager: "I do a great dael [sic]of editing in my work. Believe me—it suffers if I am tired and not up to par." (We believe you, we believe you!)

Give naps a chance

We continue to be impressed by the amount of lost productivity that non-nappers attribute to sleepiness. We could go on and on (thankfully we won't) with verbatim accounts of productivity lost to workplace sleepiness. But the bottom line is that the bottom line is being affected. And many non-nappers seem to know the solution:

- "I get grumpy when I'm tired. Sometimes a nap would definitely be worthwhile." (marketing technologist)

- "If I am sleepy at work I am unable to concentrate very well. I could benefit some days from an afternoon nap." (secretary).

- "Many engineers fall asleep at their desks involuntarily, so a nap policy would work well. I cannot concentrate and therefore cannot do my job as well as I would like." (secretary)

We also continue to be impressed by the number of companies that continue to close their eyes to what's happening in the workplace and workers' lives in general. Some employers have seen the relationship between sleepiness, napping, and productivity, but we have to be realistic: For the most part, organizational attitudes about workplace napping are still in the dark.

Somnolent saps of snoozelessness

Ever since Vice President Spiro Agnew received inordinate publicity for his alliterative attack on political opponents ("those nattering nabobs of negativity"), criticism of one's detractors carries more weight if it contains alliteration. From that perspective, we advance the phrase "somnolent saps of snoozelessness" to describe workplace napping's most strident opponents.

At times it may be necessary for nappers to be awakened and go after our opponents. And we can launch this counter-offensive against workplace napaphobes with a combination of knowledge, attitude, and skill. Knowledge is on the side of the workplace napper.

A strong attitude (nattitude) is also important. Workplace nappers have their own vocabulary of napping (see *The Art of Napping*, the companion to this book). A special vocabulary known only to workplace nappers can make those who nap at work feel part of the in crowd. *The Art of Napping* also recounts stories of famous nappers. People such as Churchill, Edison, Napoleon, and other leaders and geniuses are well-known nappers. It is helpful for workplace nappers to be aware of the larger napping community to which they belong.

Lastly, workplace nappers have to be expert nappers. Napping skills impress many people ("I wish I could do that" or "How can you nap like that?"). Naptitude (see chapter 6) is a trait that distinguishes napping folks from those unfortunates whom we know, by their attitudes, to be somnolent saps of snoozelessness.

Now there's a good workplace napping attitude

Steve tells us that he started napping at work in his early thirties because it made him feel good. When PCs were introduced into his workplace, he would find himself asleep with his fingers on the keyboard most every afternoon around 3:00 P.M. In the background he could hear a dinging sound. It was his computer; he now had several pages of garbage typed. He would shake himself awake and look around, wondering how long he had been asleep and what his last thoughts were.

Over time, he became an accomplished and public workplace napper. His workplace napping style was to pull out a desk drawer and use bubble wrap for a leg cushion. His desk was an L-shape that allowed him to rest his chair against one side and lean his head back. His napping co-workers were impressed with his napping aplomb.

Napping was an accepted practice at Steve's company—so accepted that workplace colleagues had some open fun with one another's napping prowess. On one occasion, Steve was napping at his desk during his lunch break. His office clock read 1:45. At that point a colleague sneaked into Steve's office and turned the clock ahead to 5:15. The colleague also turned the clock in the hallway ahead to 5:15. (The hallway clock hung from a 12-foot high ceiling and had to be reached with a ladder.)

Immediately after the colleague set the clocks ahead, he set the prank in motion. Another co-worker called Steve and woke him up saying: "Steve, it's 5:15 and you were supposed to drive me home—my car is in the shop Where are you? I'm standing here in my coat and figured you must have forgotten me."

Steve was discombobulated, looked at his desk clock that said 5:15, grabbed his coat and ran out into the hallway. That clock confirmed to him that it was 5:15. Maybe he did nap for four hours! He ran upstairs to his co-worker's office, and rushed in. Five men in the office chorused, "Gotcha."

z   z   z

A bed of nails would be as comfortable for napping as many workplace environments

OVERCOMING ENVIRONMENTAL BARRIERS

Beds, beds everywhere and not a nap to take

You would expect certain environments to be conducive to napping. These seemingly amenable workplaces have nap-friendly furniture nearly everywhere. A workplace napper would see hospitals, fire stations, physical therapy clinics, nursing homes, facial salons, etc., as perfect places to work. Reminders of sleep are everywhere, and the opportunity to get horizontal is ubiquitous.

Unfortunately, organizations such as these are often not nap friendly. One of the great philosophical conundrums of all time, and one that people lose sleep over both figuratively and literally is this: Why do organizations that are the most equipped with napping furniture seem to be attitudinally the least equipped to make use of the opportunity? This is indeed a question for the ages.

Our information suggests that workers in these organizations get explicit messages about what would happen if they made use of the napping furniture, and it isn't a pretty thought. Sometimes it's a written policy, other times verbal, but in all instances it's the same old tired dogma—nap and you get fired. And guess what? Employees in these firms are napping anyway, albeit secretively. In unused, unscheduled, or vacant rooms, workers are napping on these welcoming but forbidden pieces of furniture.

Nappers do find a way

The previous chapter focused on how the psychological environment at work prevents non-nappers from napping—even though many of them want to because sleepiness is affecting their productivity. This chapter looks at how workplace nappers find a way. But first, a few examples of how workplace nappers' productivity would otherwise be compromised by the sleepy-dust epidemic:

- A 26-year-old male in newspaper advertising naps because, "I am constantly under deadline pressure and when I get sluggish I miss deadlines, make errors in ad copy and that causes huge problems."

- A 41-year-old male investigator states, "I am on the road 90% of the time. I just find a quiet area to park and snooze away . . . without napping, near auto accidents have occurred several times."

- And a female project manager, age 38, says, "I have to bill my working hours out to clients; if I take a 15-minute nap break, it saves my clients money for the otherwise extended hours of staring blankly at the computer screen and calling it work."

When you read and hear, as we have, seemingly endless examples of how productivity is affected by sleepiness, and how simply it can be overcome by napping, you can't help but wonder what employers are thinking. You also have to give credit to the workplace nappers who, at risk to their jobs and/or reputation, find ways to overcome the attitudinal and architectural barriers. Workplace nappers rise above (or lay low in) nap-unfriendly work environments.

Signs of the sleepy-dust virus in the environment

Some employers are beginning to recognize the growing threat that sleepy-dust virus poses to their workplace. In some companies the virus has reached epidemic proportions, while in others it is at the incubation phase. Telltale signs are:

- Faces falling almost into the lunch plate at the cafeteria, then jerking upward—an obvious, advanced stage of the virus. Few employers miss this sign, but they often wonder what it indicates. Perhaps fine smelling cafeteria food?

- Prayer books open on many desks after lunch—unless there is another reason for a burst of religion.

- Comments of "Turn off the lights, I can't see the slides" reach crescendo proportions. Or people ask that the mission and value statement be left on the screen for 10 more minutes.

- Excessive affirmative nodding at staff meetings in which the strategic plan is being discussed—otherwise known as head bobbing when done in front of the TV.

- Too many people sitting behind the bathroom stall for too long—or male employees ask for fewer urinals and more seats.

- Closed office doors with signs saying "Do not disturb, I'm meditating." Meditation, as any napper knows, is a euphemism (napphemism) for good napping.

- People going to cars at lunch to get something and returning much later with nothing but lame explanations for what they had to have.

- Cars moving to deserted parts of the parking lot after lunch. (Yes, it *could* be for some other reason; but we prefer to think it's for private napping.)

- Drool on too many keyboards.

THE ART OF NAPPING AT WORK

Controling the spread of sleepy-dust virus

A virus spreads more quickly in unhealthy environments. In the case of *somnolentus dustus,* this virus spreads more quickly in uncomfortable environments. And uncomfortable is what many workplaces have become.

Think about some of the new office features. The omnipresent cubicle is one of the most nap-discouraging obstacles one can have. No doors, sides low enough to encourage bosses and supervisors to look over them—these were built for only the most creative of nappers. Workplace nappers tell us how they position their chair, put a phone to their ear, hold the newspaper up high, etc., all so they can nap circumspectly in their cubicle.

Fluorescent lighting is another naparaging workplace feature. Try to turn down the fluorescent light over your workspace for a more restful napping environment, and you may turn everyone's lights off and alert the whole floor to your naptime! (Not a problem if you work in Taiwan where in some workplaces the lights dim and employees put their heads on their desks for an after-lunch nap.) Expert nappers can of course nap with a spotlight in their face; but non-facilitative environments deter many potential workplace nappers from ever mastering this productivity enhancing skill.

Contrast such putative workplace advances with some nap friendly cultural innovations. The printing press (more books with which to nap), the airplane (where business people nap close together), the zipper (all the quicker to get into napping clothes), and the golf channel (no explanation needed) all have contributed to the art of napping.

The workplace napping community simply must advocate for comfortable environments to check the spread of the virus. Later, we'll see some ingenious responses being taken by some forward-looking employers.

Too busy to nap?—I don't think so

One response to the Workplace Napping Survey that routinely differentiates workplace nappers from non-nappers is this: Non-nappers often say, at times vituperatively and often strenuously, that they are "too busy" to nap. As you might expect, workplace nappers never say this. It's as if non-nappers' jobs are somehow more important and pressure packed than those of workplace nappers. This was best captured in one non-napper's haughty reply:

"I need to finish up my work so I can get home by 10 P.M." This overworked, napaphobic, 50-year-old scientist undoubtedly works all day and evening on a Nobel Prize winning project. We hope he takes a little time to nap—like Edison and Einstein often did!

Camille is never too busy to nap at work, and that's why she can be so busy and efficient. Last December, Bill tracked some of her activities, and got tired just keeping track. She was working four days a week as a fiscal manager, pulling together the company's year-end reports. She bought and wrapped over a hundred gifts for family and friends. She was serving as chairperson of the Board of Selectmen—a five-member, elected, municipal policy setting board. She became President and CFO of The Napping Company, our small family business. She hosted out of town visitors for a week, cooked meals for ten or more people half a dozen times, and, most importantly, made the holiday spirit come alive in our home.

And yes, she almost always made time for her nap.

Nappers in the closet

Many workers who are quite public about napping at home have to be secretive nappers at work. Closet nappers (or what we call clappers) are the majority of our online respondents. According to the Workplace Napping Survey, 70% of the workers who nap at work do so privately. And with good reason. Most would otherwise no longer be workers—at least with their current organization. Two issues predominate their statements.

First, they nap for productivity reasons. Napping during the break, workplace nappers believe, eliminates the productivity dip caused by sleepiness during work.

The second issue is particularly striking. Many people who do nap regularly at work expect they will be fired if found napping. Interviews and responses to the Workplace Napping Survey consistently show that workers nap at work in spite of policies that prohibit napping. They state their organizations' policy about napping at work with phrases such as:

"Absolutely No Naps"

"Sleeping on the job means immediate termination"

"Grounds for dismissal"

"No napping—period"

and variations on: *"It is an unwritten policy that napping is frowned upon."*

What we find amusing is that after quoting their employers' threatening statements, they go on to describe their own workplace napping behavior as if the company's punitive policy is irrelevant. Then they say that anywhere from one other employee to half the workforce naps at their workplace! Workplace nappers are *not* easily intimidated.

Napping out of the closet

As mentioned in *The Art of Napping,* Thomas Edison napped in and out of the closet—figuratively and literally. His assistants reported stumbling over him when he was napping in the closet, and a picture exists of him taking a very public nap on his work bench. Paradoxically, at other times he disparaged the idea of sleep altogether.

Thirty percent of our Workplace Napping Survey respondents indicate that their naps are public knowledge at the workplace. They nap openly in front of other workers or they talk openly about their workplace napping. Public napping tolerance may be a function of a more comfortable napping environment (psychologically and/or physically). It also may be due to the characteristics of the napper.

Some workplace nappers just don't care what others think of their workplace napping. They nap because they believe it is very important to their productivity, and no workplace environment is going to get in their way. In his very public endorsement of *The Art of Napping,* Jim Lehrer referred to the daily nap as "a magic bullet" for life. He practices what he preaches—closing his office door every day for an hour's nap while his assistant holds all calls.

A less famous but no less committed public napper is Cilla, who works for an orthodontist as a lab tech. Cilla naps every lunch hour for 10 minutes. The lunchroom has a table, chairs, and a couch. She puts her head on her hands at the table and wakes right up after 10 minutes of napping. Her colleagues think it's amusing, Cilla thinks it's life-enhancing. What is interesting about Cilla's story (napidote) is that she has been able to nap publicly her entire life. For example, while waiting to go on stage during her senior class play, she crawled up on the baby grand piano and took a nap! Cilla states dramatically, "A nap gives me energy, and *it's much better for me than a cup of coffee.*"

The survey says . . .

Public nappers vary greatly in how they overcome a sometimes hostile physical environment. Workplace nappers have to find a spot that was not designed for napping and stake it out as their napping spot.

For many public workplace nappers, this is the worker's lounge. Unless you are a VIP, the lounge often has the most comfortable furniture that you

THE ART OF NAPPING AT WORK

can use—designed for lounging around during breaks. It wasn't designed for napping—but, lacking a specific naproom, most workplace workers make the necessary physical adjustments. Sometimes the biggest adjustment to using the lounge as your public napping place is being able to withstand the stares and comments of workplace napaphobics, many of whom subconsciously wish they had your capacity to nap.

The next chapter discusses favorite napping places of public and private workplace nappers. What is most apparent in the survey responses and our interviews is that workplace nappers just "make do." Implicit policies that discourage, explicit polices that prohibit, uncomfortable workplace environments that complicate—none of this prevents workplace napping.

The company napnasium

Some employers have opened their eyes to what their employees are trying to tell them about the benefits of napping. These employers are designing physical environments that facilitate rather than retard productivity enhancing behavior (otherwise known as workplace napping). Their employees have voted—not with their feet but with their eyes (closed)—about what they would like their companies to do. Some companies like OP Contract in San Francisco are making sure they do the right thing. P.J. Anderson, CFO, states it perfectly, "We're very aware of the negative effects of long-term stress on the health of our staff, and on our productivity." The result has been the establishment of the "Wellness Room" outfitted with a chaise lounge, warm light, music, and the scent of lavender. Our hats and sleeping caps are off to OP Contract!

What we call a napnasium is a room specially designed to invite and facilitate workplace napping. Its environment welcomes a break. But unlike other break rooms designed for eating, drinking, talking, or smoking, this room is for napping. Terms such as wellness room, quiet room, meditation or napping area are being used by companies to describe such facilities. Microtek of Redondo Beach, California, suggests that employees on a break utilize the Library, complete with magazines, newspapers, and leather sofas for quiet or rest time.

Nap rooms often began with a different purpose in mind. Sometimes they may have been a private place for nursing mothers to express breast milk during the workday. Or sometimes they were just a vacant space that workers seized for "unofficial" napping. Whatever the original intent, these rooms were eventually re-designed for napping.

Great variability exists in how to furnish a napnasium. Should there be a cot, a mat, recliner, or couch? How much privacy should there be—one person per room or privacy screens between the nappers? Should there be a lock on the door? What other equipment might be good? How about a locker to store things, such as a pillow or blanket? Should the room be fancy and have a radio with ear plugs, towelettes, and maybe an alarm clock? And what about special situations—such as what to do about snoring in a multi-naproom? Should nap rooms be single-sex only?

All these questions make some employers' eyes roll back in their heads. Not to worry—workplace nappers are used to little or nothing when it comes to accommodations. Just ask Katrina Resevic to list the various workplace napping platforms she has utilized in her working life. She'll speak expansively of the desk bathed in the sun setting over the Charles River, the nest of drapes piled behind her video station, and the various tables and desks on or under which she has slept.

A nap room in and of itself is a tremendous breakthrough for workplace nappers. Napping accouterments for these rooms will take care of themselves over time. Sparsely furnished nap rooms are much better than none at all, as even a simply furnished room for napping gives credibility to the idea of workplace napping.

Some example napnasiums

As you might expect, napnasiums vary greatly in size and décor.

Sprint's 24-hour operations center that opened in Phoenix in 1992, for example, has a quiet room available for study or sleep. The rather spartan room contains a leather couch and a corner table. It is evident that the couch is regularly used for napping (not just studying) as the arm pillows are typically lying down. The quiet room is off a break room that has tables, puzzles, lockers, games, and food. A TV was originally in the break room, and another one was later put in the quiet room. The "quiet room" is one of many accommodations Sprint has made to address worker satisfaction.

The Pittsburgh office of Deloitte Consulting moved to new office space at Pittsburgh Plate Glass (PPG) in 1997. The majority of the firm's personnel work on the road. Employees work long hours. A napping room was designed into the new office plans from the very beginning.

The room contains a recliner with a pillow, books, and a silk flower arrangement. Its décor creates a "homey feeling." This room was originally designed for nursing mothers and is available to any employee needing to nap, close their eyes, rest, etc. The employee can use the room for as long as they need, whenever they want. The door can be locked and shades drawn if one so desires.

Not surprisingly to us, Deloitte was #8 in *Fortune* magazine's 1999 list of the best 100 Companies to Work For. With their Work/Life Balance Program as a guide, the firm recognizes that satisfied employees are more productive. There is a written policy on such features as flex time, telecommuting, reduced schedules, etc. Furthermore, money is made available for adoption assistance, and parental leave is available for both parents.

Firms that recognize the importance of workplace napping to the company and its employees also seem to take other innovative steps to enhance employee satisfaction. We will return to this theme over and over.

Architects designing nap rooms

As the workplace napping trend gathers momentum, architects will need to design napnasiums into new buildings. Yarde Metals, a Bristol, CT, metals distributor, has nap rooms on the drawing board. CEO Craig Yarde was introduced to the possibility of a napnasium after reading an article on *The Art of Napping*. Camille, Bill, and Craig met to discuss the plans.

Craig surveyed his employees on their desire to nap at work. The survey had an 80% return and he was amazed at the results. Fifty percent of the respondents said they would use a napping facility one to five times a week! Back to the drawing boards! Low lights and the soothing sounds of a waterfall are part of the napping area plans for the Bristol facility. The Philadelphia branch already is equipped with a sofa, recliners, and compact disks offering soft music for napping employees. Craig will incorporate nap rooms into the plans for the New York, New Jersey, and Boston facilities.

Craig's approach to workplace napping is a manifestation of his management philosophy. He practices "open book" management and profit-sharing, and insists that his people treat one another with equality, respect, dignity, and compassion. Anyone who hits that brick wall in the afternoon appreciates Craig's acknowledgment of the need for a nap.

Turning your individual work space into a personal napnasium

You can adapt your work space to better accommodate napping with only minor modifications. Your workstation can be your own special napnasium, designed by your own hand.

Airplanes are one of our favorite examples of a large, complex napnasium that is possible to modify. Airplanes are one of workers' favorite places to nap. Passengers begin their napping any time of the day, often during what would otherwise be considered work hours. What many passengers do not realize is that the crew finds the airplane a fine napnasium as well!

At a party, Bill was talking to two pilots and asked if they had any workplace napping napidotes. They looked at one another and remarked in unison, "Should we tell him about the paper cup?" Unable to control themselves, they told the story of a napping pilot who drooled when he napped in the cockpit. As his head dropped upon his chest, the cockpit seat would become wet with drool, detracting from the overall cockpit ambiance. Placing a paper cup between the pilot's legs to catch the drool was a simple workplace modification: It turned their workplace into a nap friendly workspace at no additional cost.

z   z   z

THE ART OF NAPPING AT WORK

Everybody needs a napping place.

FAVORITE WORKPLACE NAPPING PLACES

Waiting for the napnasium to appear

How many decades will pass before most organizations have a nap room or a nap friendly environment? Four score and ten or forty winks is as good an arbitrary answer as any. But what is a workplace napper to do in the meantime?

Workplace nappers have to create their own napping environment. Attitudinal and architectural barriers are too formidable simply to wait for acceptance and understanding from those in charge. Workplace nappers must lead the way. We can't rely on others to take up the cause. A great example is Russ Klettke of Klettke Public Relations in Chicago, for whom "a napping place is always right around the corner." The corner of a room or a walk-in closet will suffice.

Experience, either your own or your colleagues', is the source of knowledge about how to find and equip your favorite napping place. Finding it requires experimentation, both in terms of the place and the napnomics you need there. A shiftworker, for example, told us that his and his co-workers' favorite place was an unused basement room; but they were having trouble becoming comfortable with the lack of workplace napnomics in this austere environment. They solved their problem by an after-hours "requisition" of a reclining chair from the office of someone who had left the company! The shiftworkers never knew if the chair was missed, but they do know that their workplace nap is now never missed.

This chapter has suggestions from workplace nappers about favorite napping places and napnomics. Of necessity, most of these places are private. The napnomic devices—which can turn a nightmare of a site into a dream of a setting—are like most good things in life: They're free. Or as in the case of the napping shiftworkers, they're otherwise available!

Building your personal napnasium

Unlike workday exercise, workplace napping requires no personal trainer or special gym. A personal napnasium is something you build yourself in your own workplace. It can be as simple as a paper cup for your drool, or a blanket for your boss's couch! Unlike the word "personal" in exercise lexicon (e.g., personal trainer), personal here means something you do by yourself—not by employing an outside expert. And unlike gymnasium in the language of exercise, by napnasium we usually mean a place at the work site where you practice your napping, not a special workout facility. Unless you happen to be employed by Cognetics, Inc. in Cambridge, Massachusetts, where napping and exercising occur in one place. At Cognetics you can find the CEO napping in the exercise room after his noon workout.

You can develop your personal workplace napnasium without spending money. No designer clothing or expensive equipment is needed to get comfortable for a nap, and no shower is needed afterward. However, a big part of creating your special napping place is figuring out your workplace napnomics. These are a function of personal style. There are no standard requirements or special equipment such as you might need for step aerobics or weight lifting.

As a matter of fact, if you look up requirements for napping equipment on the Internet, what you'll probably find are standards used in nursery schools. For example, one standard is that a napping mat should be marked or colored so that the sleeping side can be distinguished from the floor side (probably not an important requirement for workplace napping mats). One consideration, however, concerning the following requirement may be necessary when workplace napping reaches its correct proportions: "Napping equipment shall be arranged to provide access, for each child, to a walkway without the necessity of walking on or over the cots or mats of other children." We do like that image. Would that workplace napping were so out in the open that workers had to pick their way around napping colleagues!

Some suggested workplace napnomics

When queried about favorite napping places, workplace nappers usually include a description of their napnomics with a description of the napping place. In childhood, our first napnomics allowed us to nap most anywhere. Remember the sheer terror that parents of a toddler experience when they discover that they left their two-year-old's pacifier, blanket, or teddy bear at the restaurant 100 miles back. So it is with workplace nappers and their napnomics.

The Workplace Napping Survey gives an overall picture of favorite napping places and napnomics. And in-depth interviews with workplace nappers provide detailed ideas about favorite workplace napping opportunities. Not surprisingly, many nappers who fill out the survey write that they use some item of clothing as their pillow—a jacket, sweatshirt, sweater, etc. Some workplace nappers are able to use equipment found in the workplace as a pillow. For example,

- A "middle-aged" computer worker uses a Gel keyboard.
- A 41-year-old female retail store owner uses her counter.

- A 48-year-old female musician uses her instrument case.

- A 34-year-old funeral director/embalmer uses a pillow from the casket. (He says it's always an unused one.)

- A waiter, no age given, uses a tablecloth and napkins. (He didn't say whether they were used or not—and we prefer not to know.)

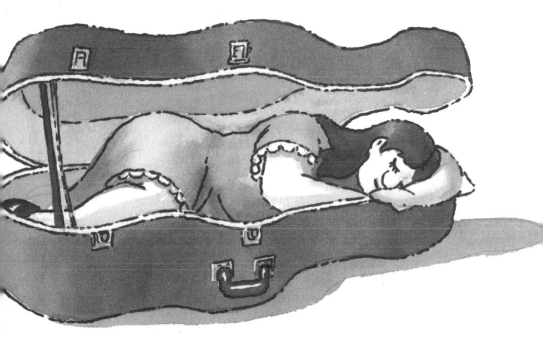

Perhaps the most unusual workplace napnomic is a roll of toilet paper (more about that later).

Some more napnomics

Many workplace nappers pay close attention to simple things that increase their napping comfort—particularly the light, heat, and sounds in their personal napping environment.

- A female customer service representative, age 25, was very specific: "I put my head on my desk and cover my head with a coat, sweatshirt, sweater, etc. I have my alarm on my watch set . . ."

- A female bureau manager (no age given) says her screen saver makes "quiet bubble sounds" which she considers a great napnomic.

- A 40-year-old female physician says the soft music in her office is a perfect napnomic.

- A 35-year-old pharmacy manager finds the noise from the fan "soothing."

- In contrast, a 42-year-old research associate says his most important napnomics by far are earplugs.

Blankets, shawls, afghans, etc., are often mentioned as a simple way to control room temperature. Still other napnomics are used to set the mood for napping. There's nothing like reading a company report:

- A female credit analyst, age 28, advised us: "Napping is not allowed;

however, when the time is right, pull out a good report, pretend you're reading it, and it's nighty-night time."

Diversionary napnomics

There is a special class of napnomics used by employees who must nap privately. Diversionary napnomics assist a napper, not to nap more successfully, but to nap more secretly. The majority of workplace nappers still must engage in workplace napping as if it were sinful rather than helpful, and as a result some have raised napping to a high art form.

People in occupations as varied as prison guard, crane operator, warehouse worker, health care workers of all types, business professionals, teachers, etc., have informed us of how they nap secretly. Indeed, we can't think of any occupation that couldn't be configured so one could nap secretly. Typical diversionary napnomics are turning your back and putting a phone to your ear or a paper in front of your eyes.

The essence of diversionary napnomics is to make it look like you are working when in actuality you are napping. The question remains whether you are fooling anyone, or primarily helping yourself to believe that no one notices. The important point is that they seem to work, i.e., diversionary napnomics allow workers to feel they are napping circumspectly. For example,

- A consumer risk analyst, male, age 29, puts his back to the hallway and naps at his desk with reports spread out over the desk.

Company reports and other types of company correspondence actually are dual-purpose napnomics. They get you in the mood to nap because they are typically long and boring; then you keep them in front of you to try and disguise your nap, as if you were actually using them! Let workplace nappers question no longer the value of a strategic planning document.

Other examples of diversionary napnomics are:

- When the weather turns cold, preventing outdoor napping, a 32-year-old female technical writer goes to the library, opens a book, and naps without reading a sentence.

- Speaking of weather, a 48-year-old weather forecaster retires from view ostensibly to study the latest computer printouts.

- A 38-year-old female marketing manager proudly wrote that she puts a pen in her hand and lays her head on her desk: "I can go from asleep to alert in the millisecond it takes for someone to walk into the room."

Even workers who can nap in some privacy arrange their nap environment to hide the fact that they are napping. For example,

- An information specialist, female, age 28, went into some detail: "I pull out a few drawers, lean my chair against one and put my feet on the other; then with two small pillows from home, I lean my head back on my chair and cross my arms. It's not the most comfortable position, but it is easy to recover from if someone should knock on my door."

While some workers rest their head on their briefcase, The Company Store, a catalogue store featuring fine bed furnishings, has taken this idea a head bob further. They now sell an executive napping briefcase, complete with a pillow for napping and a copy of *The Art of Napping*.

Workplace napping platforms

Napping platforms are what support your body while you are napping. The most popular workplace napping platform is a chair, preferably one that tilts backward.

At Circadian Technologies, a leader in solving problems of fatigue and poor alertness in companies that function around the clock, we used a prototype of a high-tech napping chair manufactured by a Japanese firm. If you are a high-tech person, this lounge chair with fans and lights to awaken you will make your napping a first-class experience.

A surprising number of workplace nappers nap on the floor, some using exercise mats, others simply finding a carpeted floor. Laying your head on your desk and using your hands for a pillow is also common. Putting a soft chair in a meeting room is for a napper like putting a bone in front of a dog. They are both gone within minutes.

Some workers take advantage of equipment that resembles a napping platform (although, as we mentioned before, employers with nap friendly furniture tend to act like nap police).

- A female physical therapist in her 30s noted that the treatment table in the room furthest from the reception area is not routinely scheduled for patients and does serve as an unofficial napping platform for therapists.

- A 40-year-old male laborer who works outdoors reported that he and several of his colleagues nap on wooden benches and picnic tables.

- Several nursery school teachers have said they use an extra napping rug to nap while the kids are napping.

- A 41-year-old graphic designer retreats to the supply room and naps on the matte cutting table, using bubble wrap for a pillow.

Favorite public places to nap

Favorite public places to nap are less popular than private ones, because workers have to know that their job is not in jeopardy if they nap publicly. As mentioned in chapter 4, far and away the most popular public spot is the lounge or cafeteria. In many workplaces there seems to be an implicit, unwritten policy that lounge napping is okay. For some companies, desk napping is also tolerated: as one woman was told by her boss, "Just don't flaunt it." We've never come across a "nap flaunting" policy, but we assume not flaunting means that you don't take off your makeup and get in your pajamas. Anything else would seem appropriate, at least to us.

Even people who purport to be non-nappers have found themselves napping in staff meetings or in-service programs. For nappers, the primary justification for an afternoon meeting is a satisfying afternoon nap.

- A female physician told us that the length of her afternoon naps depends on "how long the boring meeting is." She says, "Napping is better than what's going on in the meeting." She says she is able to stay "awake" enough while napping to participate in the meeting if she needs to make a point. (More on this advanced practice in the final chapter.)

Another overwhelming favorite place to nap is outdoors. People who work outdoors in pleasant temperatures simply find a spot to lie down.

- A 26-year-old female archaeologist says she sits on her screen to nap.

How public or private the nap is depends upon how far from work one ventures outdoors to nap. Some nappers are able to drive or walk to a park or park-like setting. Some nappers who nap inside try to pretend they are outside—by using napping equipment associated with the outdoors. Some roll out camping mats or beach towels on their office floor.

- A 49-year-old plant manager brings his own lawn chair into his office for napping. He thinks he is out by the lake.

Favorite private places to nap

Many people who drive to work nap in their cars during the workday. Could this be why some people avoid public transportation? If the bus were available for afternoon napping in the parking lot more people would take it!

What surprises us is that while so many people nap in their cars at work, they often think they are the only ones carnapping. Perhaps carnappers are too tired to notice carnapping colleagues? Carnappers nap where they park, or drive to a more private spot on or off company grounds. The car radio, an open window, a comforter, pillow, or a baseball cap pulled low over the eyes have all been reported as napnomics that add to carnapping reverie.

As a group, carnappers are primarily in their 20s and early 30s. Lacking in seniority, maybe they also lack private offices or the confidence to nap in public at work. Certainly they take advantage of reclining car seats. Comfortable, reclining car seats are one of the greatest nap-friendly innovations of this century.

Another favorite place to nap is the company bathroom. Stallnappers also think they are the only ones napping there—and we must admit that until the Workplace Napping Survey was put online, we had not heard of it. Now people call in radio talk shows and tell us about how they nap in the bathroom—as a British napper (we assume) said, "I nap in the ladies loo." People have truly come out of the closet (water closet) when it comes to stallnapping. Stallnapping does have advantages: The door can be secured, you can stay as long as you like, you won't be interrupted, and few people will suspect you are napping. And the toilet paper roll should always be available as a napnomic.

- A 31-year-old female project manager wrote, "Because I have to hide my naps, I end up sitting on the toilet with my head on the toilet paper roll. Glamorous, eh?"

THE ART OF NAPPING AT WORK

- As far as we know a business executive in his mid-40s holds the record for stallnapping. While attending a meeting in another country, and still suffering from jet lag, he excused himself from the meeting. He went to the men's room and stallnapped for 1 $\frac{1}{2}$ hours.

Napping on the boss's couch

Camille napped on her boss's couch in her previous job, and people were amazed. Bill named a nap after her—the Camille Nap, considered the most brazen of all naps. We knew it was unusual when *The Today Show* taped her napping in her boss's office, and other media people interviewed her about her workplace napping practice. Of all the Workplace Napping Surveys filled out so far, only one other person has said they nap on the boss's couch.

If it isn't popular, then why is the Camille Nap so intriguing? We think it's because the Camille Nap has some positive napping features that many workplace nappers envy. First of all, this type of nap has the boss's blessing. There is no better guilt-free napping experience at the workplace. In the boss's office, the couch and the surroundings are as good as it gets in the organization. The Camille Nap also gets the respect of other workers, because the person in charge has countenanced it. Finally when the boss has a Camille Nap going on, a workplace napper knows that napping has arrived as a legitimate company benefit.

Rating workplace naps

Some naps stand out for the uniqueness of the napping setting or for the creative use of napnomic devices. A number of napidotes describe napping behavior that we find particularly compelling and would rate as tens on the ten-point workplace napping degree-of-difficulty scale.

- A 49-year-old dentist who has his own office permits workplace napping for staff and himself. At lunchtime he descends to the basement for a 30 to 60 minute nap using a mattress and pillow that he has placed there permanently. His napnomic device to wake up is particularly impressive. When his staff "turn on the air system for the suction" to get the equipment ready for the afternoon appointments, the sound awakens him. It works better than an alarm and his staff do not have to wake him up.

- A female workplace napper told a story about her ex-husband that rates high for uniqueness of the setting and creative use of napnomics— although very low on safety. It seems that every night at work he would go into the men's room, pull down his pants and sit on the toilet to nap. He would lean back on the rolls of toilet paper stacked behind the toilet. It gets even more interesting. He would then light a cigarette, put it between his fingers close to his hand and bare leg, and begin his nap. When the cigarette burned down and he felt its heat, that would wake him up. He said this took about 15 minutes and was very refreshing!

Rating co-workers' and friends' naps and sharing napidotes is an enjoyable way to spend one's work break; it can get you in the mood for napping at the next break. If you wish to share napidotes with the larger napping community, fill out the Workplace Napping Survey (online at www.napping.com). Who knows you could be on Candid Napping!

Favorite napping places and your job choice

It occurred to us while we were napping that maybe someone could put napping questions on a vocational interest test! The idea would be that your preference for certain napping places is factored into the test's determination of the job in which you might be most interested. Following are sample napping preference test items and jobs such a preference might suggest.

Napping in the dark: night watchmen, politicians from the other party

Napping in cramped spaces: truck drivers, funeral directors

Napping off the road: salespeople, policemen

Napping on padded tables: physical therapists, athletes, wrestlers

Talking while other people are napping: college professors; clergy

Napping at 500 miles an hour: airline pilots

Napping in a snake pit: lawyers (had to have a lawyer joke!)

Napping during a presidential election: most American workers

Napping while others work

In addition to professors and clergy, other occupations work with napping customers. Musicians and actors sometimes work for napping customers— but unfortunately for them, probably not for too long. Except for their own pilots, airlines prefer to have nappers on their planes. Napping customers don't eat, drink, or complain—at least while they're napping.

We wonder about the current growth of services such as massage, yoga, and facials. We think that one of the draws to these services is the opportunity to nap while receiving other health benefits. We would *advertise* the napping opportunities inherent in these services.

And what about new services that could make a living renting napping platforms? We think people would be willing to pay rent for napping platforms in airports, bus stations, train stations, interstate rest stops, amusement parks, restaurants, bars, etc. We need to increase the availability of napping platforms, and make napping products and services a separate industry. Just like peace, let's give napping a chance.

z   z   z

Doing what comes naturally—
only doing it at work.

A WORKPLACE NAPPING PRIMER

So what does "out" mean?

When one isn't working during the workday one is typically said to be "out": i.e., "out to lunch," "out of the office," or just "out." Workers who can't hone their napping skills publicly might want to use the word "out" as their naphemism for napping at work.

Many workplace nappers are already doing so. When they tell their bosses, colleagues, etc., that they'll be "out" for a while, they mean as in "lights out"! Should their communication be misinterpreted as "out to a meeting," "out to lunch," or otherwise "unavailable" because of some pressing work matter, then so be it.

As a useful variation on "out," we are impressed by how the term "flat out" can conjure up the image of a harried, intense worker—even when actually used to mean horizontal napping. Two fathers gleefully told us that when their wives returned from shopping (the husbands had been instructed to watch the kids) they dutifully reported to their wives that they had been "flat out" with the kids. The husbands proudly shared with us that they had reported honestly and that they indeed had been "flat out"—"flat out" on their couches.

Developing your naptitude

Whether you're a public or private workplace napper, whether your lunch break is really also a nap break, whether "out of the office" means you're napping in your car, most people can improve their workplace napping experience. The tricks of the trade are becoming known as more people talk about their exploits. Workplace nappers are by nature very sharing people.

This chapter is a mine of workplace napping tips. In a burst of originality (following a nap), and as a tribute to Steven Covey's book, we called these trade secrets "seven habits of highly effective workplace nappers." Habits, of course, are not something you think about every time you nap. Initially, while you're incorporating some of these ideas into your own

Good

Better

napping style, you may wish to focus on them. Eventually they'll become natural to your routine.

You may already be practicing many of these seven habits. Some people diagnose themselves as missing just one of the habits; and once they master that one, workplace napping becomes more productive and satisfactory for them. Here are the seven habits of highly effective workplace nappers:

1. Announce your nap to yourself and if possible to your colleagues.

For many people, this is the key step to guilt free, productive workplace napping. To feel comfortable psychologically when napping, you have to know that you are doing yourself and your company a favor. By "announcing" your nap to yourself, you are reinforcing and reminding yourself of its productivity and health benefits. Many non-nappers who admit to productivity problems due to sleepiness remain napless because they haven't given themselves permission to nap. As a result they're missing out on one of life's simple pleasures. Expert workplace nappers of course experience no such angst.

- A 29-year-old self-employed woman reports that when she feels ready to nap she says to herself something like this: "Are you tired? Maybe you're getting sick . . . better lie down and rest."

Many individuals simply close a door to a room (their office or a vacant room) and nap. The closed door is how they let others know that they are napping. Some put a post-it on their door, or some other sign announcing that a nap is in progress.

- We particularly like the sign used by a Great Lakes Ship Master and Pilot, obviously a former Navy man: "Nooner in progress. Do not disturb."

Other individuals are not only open about it by napping publicly, they make sure their colleagues know that napping is an important part of who they are.

- A 37-year-old female video editor says: "I'm the insistent eccentric; not only does napping help me with my work, but it fosters my reputation as different, and therefore an artist!"

Most workplace nappers aren't eccentric, but how you present your napping to others will influence how they perceive it. We suggest that no matter to whom you announce your nap (colleagues or just yourself), do it in a matter-of-fact manner, with a hint of pride and satisfaction.

2. Gather your napnomic devices

This much we know: every workplace napper has devices that make his or her nap more pleasurable. Often these napnomic devices are discovered step by step, like a child might build with blocks. Sooner or later workplace nappers have developed their own napping equipment, tailored to themselves and their workplace idiosyncrasies. If they can't leave their workplace napmomics at the work site, they can transport them in their own unique work napsack.

We are impressed with how proud workplace nappers are of their napnomics. Some have specially crocheted shawls or afghans. Others have favorite pillows. We are also impressed with how workplace nappers make sure that other workers have napnomics they might like. Camille's co-workers bought her a blanket to use for her naps on her boss's couch.

- A 40-year-old female benefits administrator said that she "brought in a folding lawn chair and equipped it with a pillow and blanket. It is for two of our pregnant employees." However her actions weren't entirely altruistic. "But I sneak onto it too! I sure wish I had such an arrangement five years ago when I was pregnant. I had to nap on a very small loveseat."

3. Ensure a method for on-time awakening

Many expert workplace nappers don't worry about awakening from their nap. They just do. Our eccentric video editor sounded a common theme:

- "I sleep in 20-minute intervals. And I keep at it! Practice makes perfect. I can now fall asleep easily and wake up easily, because I do it often."

Concern about on-time awakening can ruin a good nap. Workplace nappers who are apprehensive about waking up on time use wristwatch, clock, or radio alarms. Some use colleagues or fellow nappers who take turns awakening one another when it's time. Of course, it is sometimes impossible to remove all the dangers, especially if napping is a secret workplace practice.

- A woman (no age or occupation given) told of her attempts to manage her on-time awakening: "I e-mailed a friend of mine and asked her to call me in twenty minutes, as I was going to lay my head down on my desk for a few minutes. The phone rang 20 minutes later and I woke up in my nap-time drool and said 'Thanks Mandy, man I feel better.' It was my boss. OOOOpppps. He was calling from out of town. . . . I really had to double-step to keep him from figuring out I'd been asleep. But I tell you what, I felt so much better."

And danger is what workplace napping pilots have, especially if they're all napping together—Who will wake them up?! In one incident that has become a classic, a transcontinental cargo flight overshot Los Angeles and flew for another hour over the Pacific before air traffic controllers could awaken the crew: a compelling example of the importance of ensuring a method for on time awakening!

4. Ensure control of your nap environment, including a plan to avoid nappus interruptus

Nappers need to feel secure in their nap, knowing not only that they have a method to wake up, but also that they will not be awakened prematurely (i.e., experience *nappus interruptus*).

Common strategies are to shut off the phone, hold calls, find an out-of-the-way or secret napping spot, close the door, and/or use a sign indicating a nap in progress. Some people don't use a napping sign because napaphobic colleagues would see the sign as an invitation to knock on the door and ruin the nap. (Must be a reflection of "nap envy," which napaphobics express in subliminal, childish ways.)

We particularly like the confidence one prison guard has about avoiding nappus interruptus.

- A 54-year-old male prison guard stated matter-of-factly: "I nap at my desk during lockdown time. . . . My supervisor cannot get to me without a co-worker letting him/her into my area. My co-worker would advise me before letting the supervisor into my area."

Fellow co-workers are often enlisted to help keep the environment nap friendly during a colleague's nap. And where there are enough people napping in public, napaphobics wouldn't even think about waking a napper. In these nap-popular work environments, pesky napaphobics disappear like mosquitoes in bright sunlight—they dare not be exposed.

- A 55 year-old library assistant says five of her colleagues nap, and "when someone is lying down in the lounge, they are never disturbed."

Nap etiquette is alive and well in environments with a critical mass of nappers:

- A female bureau manager (no age given) reports that ten of her colleagues nap, and that "if my colleagues see me lying on my desk, they'd understand not to wake me, and I would do the same for them."

Nappus interruptus can still occur in settings where many people nap but company policy forbids it. Such a situation can reduce one's napping pleasure.

- A laboratory worker, age 44, who believes that 15–30 of her co-workers nap without the company's blessing, says she has "no devices to prevent interruption. I take my chances and hide behind the newspaper and try to pull myself together if anyone takes me by surprise."

Some nappers make it perfectly clear that they are not to be interrupted while napping.

- A 44-year-old self-employed female states: "Everyone knows I've been napping all my life, and I give people very firm instructions: Don't bother me when I'm napping unless there is an absolute emergency—like a fire or medical emergency. . . . I am bold and blatant in my napping and, yes, the lessons I learned in kindergarten have served me well: When you're tired, take a nap."

5. Revel in the nap

Enjoy! No relevant suggestions here if you master the other six habits.

THE ART OF NAPPING AT WORK

6. Deal with sleep inertia, if necessary

Sleep inertia is that groggy, slightly disorienting feeling that some nappers experience when awakening. Nonapapologists believe that if you nap about 40–60 minutes you'll be waking up from a deep sleep and more apt to experience sleep inertia. To combat sleep inertia they recommend naps of shorter duration (20–30 minutes) or longer duration (90–100 minutes). They also say to refrain from making critical decisions immediately after waking up from a deep sleep.

The ability to deal with sleep inertia is what separates proficient workplace nappers from wannabes. Experienced nappers know that the effects of sleep inertia are usually short-lived, while the benefits of napping last throughout the workday. Some nappers just "shake off" the effects of sleep inertia. Others have developed certain strategies:

> *"I have to get up and walk around and get the blood circulating to try to overcome it," says a 36-year-old male software engineer.*

> *"I check e-mail before getting back to work," reports a 30-year-old economist.*

> *"I need to give myself a few minutes to get adjusted," writes a 32-year old female accounting clerk.*

> *"Drink coffee" is the simple instruction of a 54-year-old, male personnel manager.*

> *"I find a cup of coffee after a good nap to be quite refreshing,"* opines
> a 42-year-old male research associate.

> *"I stop at the washroom (which is conveniently on the way to my
> cube) and wash my face,"* says a 21-year-old male electrical
> engineer who naps off-site.

Some people seem to do it all.

- A 29-year-old proposal writer writes in proposal level detail: "I go to the
  ladies room, splash water on my face, brush my hair and put in eye
  drops, walk around, and get some water or coffee."

Some people don't do anything.

- A 32-year-old female technical writer is anything but technical: "I wake
  up 'bright eyed and bushy tailed'."

As the examples show, overcoming sleep inertia isn't rocket science. For
the most part all the things you need are readily available: water, coffee, a
bathroom, and a good nattitude.

7. Begin to plan your next nap as you awaken from this nap

Even accomplished nappers often miss this step. But it is important to make
napping opportunities part of your daily planning, even if you don't always
use the opportunity.

It is not unusual to plan the next time for a pleasurable or needed activity while you're still participating in the activity. Camille plans her next meal

while eating her current meal; golfers plan the next golf day, skiers the next ski run, walkers the next walk, etc., as part of finishing up.

Planning your next nap gives you the chance to add new features, make changes in your routine, and critique your present napping style. Furthermore, planning your next nap while awakening from your current one reinforces the importance of scheduling time for napping and remembering its importance in your work life.

Shiftworkers who work long shifts, rotating shifts, or night shifts particularly need to plan their napping routine. They are often sleep deprived and nap secretly anyway.

- A 36-year-old factory shiftworker plans his next workplace nap around his rotating schedule: "We work 12-hour shifts which we change day to night after every day off we have, so you can't help but nap." He naps "around 3 A.M. behind large objects," and reports that about 75% of his colleagues nap as well.

Telenapping for telecommuters

The seven habits of highly effective workplace napping are easily practiced by those who work at home. We speak of the six turn-ons to telenapping:

Turn away from work	*Turn off the phone*
Turn up the radio	*Turn over the pillow*
Turn down the blanket	*Turn in—for a nap*

Some telenappers still feel guilty about napping at home. When you call them on the phone and they have been napping, many will deny it. When family members come home from work and school, do telenappers swell with napping pride and speak openly of their napping even when there's no need to go public? We don't think so. Telecommuters practice telenapping more than they talk about it. But the flexibility to arrange a napping schedule makes telenappers the envy of the workplace napping community.

- A 34-year-old male writer says haughtily that he makes his own nap policy: "Since I am working at home I sort of do what I want. I sleep when I feel like it."

Some individuals work so close to their home that they are reviving the siesta culture.

- A 65-year-old physician goes home, naps for 30 minutes, and "if somebody calls my wife takes the call."

- A 35-year-old electronics manager states: "I go home at lunch to eat and then have a 15–20 minute nap."

A short commute and a short nap—does it get any better than that? Not according to Priscilla Dwyer of Carpe Diem Games® in Reading, MA. As a lifelong napper, she continues the practice when she is tired and unable to focus on the task at hand. Creativity is an essential ingredient in designing the award-winning children's and family card games manufactured by Carpe Diem, and napping does enhance it.

Work, family, and napping

It's a fact of life: Working parents will beg and grovel for napping opportunities. How much would new parents pay for the opportunity to nap when they wish? Is the two-income family the no-nap family?

We recommend that new parents hire a babysitter, not so they can go out, but so they can stay home—and nap. Childrearing is the most important job there is. Like telecommuting, it involves working at home. Yet parents (particularly mothers) are often too guilty about what else they should be doing around the house to take advantage of the rare napping opportunity when it presents itself.

When young children nap, that's the time for one or both parents to nap as well. Laundry, cleaning, yardwork, etc., are not as important as a rested parent. When Bill was home with his children when they were small, he always tried to nap with his kids—"quality time," he called it, for all of them! When the children were about ready to give up their naps, Bill napped longer than they did. Just because the kids were giving up their afternoon nap for a while, Bill didn't think he should—and he never did!

Eight advantages of workplace napping

As people become more effective workplace nappers, they begin to see the advantages that workplace napping has over other types of activities. We can think of eight, and named them the eight advantages of workplace napping.

Workplace napping:

Makes you feel better (enhances your mood)

Makes you more productive (increases your performance)

Is inexpensive (won't cost you a cent)

Is a no-sweat activity (no shower needed, and it won't wear out your joints)

Is self-prescribed (a doctor's orders are not necessary)

Is not an invasive procedure (no one needs to do anything to you)

Is not fattening (no weight gain—you can't eat when you are asleep)

Has no dangerous side effects (as long as you aren't driving)

With so many advantages for the worker and the company, it's hard to believe that employers won't change policy to make workplace napping as acceptable as the lunch break and the coffee break.

z   z   z

THE ART OF NAPPING AT WORK

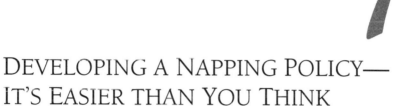

Bosses and supervisors hold the key to the employee naproom.

DEVELOPING A NAPPING POLICY—
IT'S EASIER THAN YOU THINK

It's time for a policy change

Let's reiterate facts that lead unequivocally to a change in policy:

> *Workers nap at work to become more productive.*

> *Workplace napping is grounds for dismissal or discipline.*

> *Many workers are napping at work anyway.*

The current policy on napping might best be called the Swiss cheese napping policy—foreign to what's really going on and full of holes. Employers

103

have missed the productivity reasons for napping and mistakenly believe that workers wish to sleep on the job, rather than nap at the work site. The traditional anti-napping argument is most adamantly stated by employers as: "We're not paying people to sleep—they can do that someplace else." But their heads are stuck so far down in the sand that their speech is garbled.

Is anyone listening?

Many workers can't nap productively because of implicit or explicit napping policies. Our Workplace Napping Survey asks workers if they would be willing to approach their boss about a policy change; almost all say they would not. Some elaborate:

- A 24-year-old female editorial assistant wrote, "If my company had a room that had a couch and a door with a sign that read, 'Do not disturb, employee sleeping,' I would love it!"

- An information specialist, age 32, says his company's policy is not very informative and he'd rather not ask about it. "It's not written. No one has complained. Not all the bosses know that people nap. So we try to be discrete, not knowing if they would approve or not."

- Taking a page from the defense department, a 36-year-old male software engineer stated, "I follow a don't ask-don't tell policy."

- Other workplace nappers see napping as a place where one can pull rank. A 46-year-old graphic designer wrote, "There is not really a nap policy. I just started doing it because I was nodding out at my computer after lunch. With a certain amount of seniority in my favor, no one has really objected."

- Some very confident workplace nappers take the lack of an explicit policy as an invitation to nap. A 33-year-old male researcher who naps publicly was adamant: "There is no policy that I am aware of and I don't care."

The nap starts here —at the top

Both employees and employers have concerns about workplace napping. They worry that the company will be publicly embarrassed if they have an explicit nap-friendly policy. Pejorative phrases such as "Company X caught napping" or "Company Y asleep at the switch" might find their way into headlines. (Napaphobics are so trite and unimaginative!) Some companies who speak about their nap-friendly policies do so only on the condition of anonymity.

Anonymity is not an issue with David Birch, CEO of Cognetics, a 16-year-old, Cambridge-based consulting/software firm (the boss who naps publicly in the company's exercise room). David has always encouraged his employees to follow his example.

David has exercised and napped at work since he began at MIT as a lab director. Now he exercises and then lies down on a mat for 10–15 minutes each day. Employees in the room don't interfere with his nap and don't bother him. He uses no napnomics other than the mat, and he wakes up automatically.

David says that by having a break in the middle of the day, he has two mornings. As 80% of his work is accomplished in the morning, he can double his output! "It is like starting a whole new day," he reports.

And for those who aren't "morning people," workplace napping gives a second chance at getting the morning right! If you didn't do well in the PN morning, maybe you'll like the feel of the AN morning!

Changing the workplace culture from anti-nap to pro-nap

Some companies haven't thought much about a nap policy. Change to a nap friendly policy in these companies wouldn't be nearly as difficult as in explicitly anti-napping ones.

Anti-napping is exactly what the Burlington Northern Santa Fe Railway *was*, according to Al Lindsey, General Director of Safety and Rules. The military was instrumental in developing the railroads, and military culture still reigned when it came to napping—you could be fired for napping at work. But in 1992, the company started a discussion of fatigue and safety issues. Educational materials and consultation from the NASA Ames Research Center convinced them in 1996 that the time had come to institute a napping policy.

The material about fatigue, safety, and napping was presented to the chief operating staff. Meetings with local union leaders described the new policy and asked for input. Labor put together their own pamphlet explaining the new policy.

When the new policy was first implemented on the Arizona line, it failed. It instructed train crews to call in to get permission to nap, and the crews felt that they were being made fun of when they called in. A simpler policy was initiated on other lines: No call-in was required, the nap could be no longer than 45 minutes, and one person must be awake.

Now train and engine crews have a napping policy. Al says education was the key to culture change. People at all levels needed to be educated on the natural, normal benefits of napping.

Note well that the policy became successful when it was simple and based on trust. Excessive monitoring can stifle the implementation of a nap policy. Just imagine if your bathroom breaks were monitored: It would be like junior high school all over again.

Napping policy as a company benefit

Can't you just envision a company-benefits person explaining benefits to a new worker, i.e., the company retirement plan, the health plan, the vacation package, and the *napping benefit?* Well, imagine no more you sleepy heads, it's already happening at some very good companies.

Susie Campolong is a benefits administrator at Deloitte Consulting, which as previously indicated has a room for napping. She makes sure that new

hires see the napping facility while on their tour of the company, and she encourages employees to use it. She knows the room is well used but because they don't monitor napping, she doesn't know a statistic. Susie says: "There's no down side to the firm's napping policy; it is only beneficial." She has heard of no problems associated with use of the napping room.

Susie also knows first-hand the productivity benefits of her company's napping policy. She suffers regularly from severe migraine headaches, and uses the napping room when early symptoms appear. She needs a dark, quiet room to decrease the severity of the pain. The rest makes it bearable for her to continue her workday, even though the headache may last for 24 hours.

We also like how telenappers state their own nap policy—so simple and straightforward:

- A 33-year-old, female, public relations consultant/freelance writer took great delight in telling us her nap policy. "I'm self-employed and work out of a home office. My policy is: The more naps the better!" And she adds: "At my former workplace (large credit card bank), napping would have been seriously frowned upon. I occasionally stole a nap with my head on my desk."

Will new companies lead the nap policy trend?

Yes, many established organizations are converting to nap friendly policies. But we can't help but be impressed with relatively new companies that accept napping as part of corporate culture from their very inception. We sometimes wonder if their enlightened attitude is due to these new CEOs being closer in years to their college experience. They haven't forgotten one of the most important life-lessons they learned at college: Napping can make you more productive.

Working out of their dorm rooms, in December 1995 six college students from Yale and Columbia started Student.net, an Internet publishing company. The company's deadlines require long hours, and napping has always been part of the culture. The company has flexible work schedules, and employees dress however they want. A couch and two oversized chairs in the waiting area are used for napping.

Nobody asks permission to nap, and certainly not employee Eric Ng. All Eric's friends know he naps, and he says proudly, "I am absolutely a napper." He began in high school but napped more extensively at Yale. Eric worked summers in companies where he couldn't nap, but has always napped at Student.net (his first full time position). He shares an office with Kevin. The couch in their office is a comfy, full-sized sofa with side pillows. Anyone in the firm is welcome to come in and nap on the couch at anytime.

Eric says, "Napping refreshes me and gives me my second wind for the day." He arrives at 8:30 to 9:00 A.M. and doesn't leave until 9:00 P.M. It's a long day and he naps when he "no longer feels sharp."

THE ART OF NAPPING AT WORK

Industries leading the napping trend

In addition to newer industries led by younger CEOs (e.g., computer, Internet, communications), some established industries are considering nap-friendly policies. The transportation industry—railroads, trucking, and airlines—is a prime example. They have a lot to lose in lives and equipment if employees are sleep deprived when working.

If, for example, you're a train crew member "working on the railroad" for Union Pacific, since March 1998 you have been working for managers who are on the right track about workplace napping. The train crew policy allows one of the crew to nap up to 45 minutes, as long as the train is stopped, secure, and safe. Benefits to Union Pacific of this policy include improved employee morale, enhanced alertness and productivity, and a greater trust in management that could think outside the box. (Until March 1998, napping at the job meant termination.)

Also interested in rolling out napping policies are health care organizations. Again, the stakes are high if mistakes are made. One example of potential risks due to *somnolentus dustus* running rampant through a hospital: It has been reported that performance of sleep-deprived surgeons is impaired similarly to that of motorists driving drunk.

As more and more businesses provide services 24 hours a day, 7 days a week, employees must work either rotating shifts or fixed night shifts. Such industries need to pay special attention to napping strategies for their workers to remain productive and healthy.

As more organizations see the productivity and health benefits of workplace napping, the trend will be toward nap-friendly policies. As increasing numbers of industries break ranks with their less tolerant brethren, they will break bread with those who advocate the benefits of workplace napping.

This policy won't fly for long

According to *Shiftwork* magazine, a flight attendant once found the entire cockpit crew asleep. That flight attendant now makes it a habit to check in on the crew every half-hour to make sure someone is awake! In another airline napidote, a pilot reported that on one flight, both the first officer and the captain were sound asleep 25 minutes after departure.

The truth is, many pilots are napping—sometimes called "unofficial and uncontrolled cockpit napping." Whether there is a policy or not, pilots often take turns napping—a tag team practice certainly preferable to collective cockpit napping.

Napping research has shown that napping during flight helps pilots to be more alert at the critical takeoff and landing phases. As a result, some airlines are already encouraging pilots to nap in the cockpit ("controlled cockpit rest," naphemistically). With three-member crews, pilots are even allowed to rotate out of the cockpit and nap in a cabin seat on long flights.

Soon, airline policies will be more nap friendly—in the interest of safety and enhanced crew performance. Whether passengers (many of whom are also napping) will ever be aware of this policy is unknown.

"This is the captain speaking. While my co-pilot is flying the plane, I will join you in a mid-flight nap. Happy napping!"

Working when I should be sleeping—and vice versa

Some 20% of us work at night when we should be sleeping. People on night shifts nap at work whether the employer admits it or not.

Night workers have already implemented an unofficial nap policy. The question for employers is, "Do you want to formalize the policy, so that workers who wish to nap can nap guilt-free and get more napping productivity benefits? Or, do you wish to remain out of touch with what your workers are doing to enhance their productivity?"

They aren't out of touch in Saskatoon. At Siecor's manufacturing plant in Saskatchewan, the night shift can nap up to 20 minutes in the employees' lounge. The napping platform is in a designated quiet area complete with couches, easy chairs, music, and low lights. This policy was instituted along with other benefits for night shiftworkers—including free fruits and vegetables, an exercise room for work breaks, and a library of information on diet, sleep, and shiftworker coping strategies.

In essence, shiftworkers and their employers need to arrive at a compromise: "I work during part of my sleep time, and you let me sleep during part of your work time."

Our policy on policies

Our policy on policies is to keep policy simple. Bosses and supervisors initially worry about napping being one more thing to monitor. We remind them that no additional monitoring is needed.

A napping policy allows workers to nap on their breaks. If employers now monitor break time, then they can continue to do so, but they don't need to monitor the practice of napping itself. Unless of course they already monitor how much people eat at the lunch break, smoke at the smoke break, drink at the water cooler and coffee breaks, and at the bathroom break how much . . . We don't think we need to go there!

A napping policy is simple: "Nap on your break if you wish. Workplace napping is your individual decision, and won't affect your reputation one way or the other."

THE ART OF NAPPING AT WORK

Will napping at the workplace be followed by napping while working?

THE FUTURE OF WORKPLACE NAPPING

Common sense isn't common anymore

If workers are falling asleep on the job, or are unproductive because of sleepiness, common sense says that changes are in order. But common sense isn't common when it comes to workplace napping.

Starting now, more and more workers will be asking their bosses a simple question: "Why can't I nap, without guilt or fear, on my break time?" And the common sense answer will be, "You can." Starting now, more and more bosses and supervisors will ask themselves, "Why not use workplace napping as a no-cost way to improve worker productivity and morale?" And the common sense answer will be, "We will."

The immediate workplace policy change is to allow (encourage) napping during breaks. The not too distant change will be to accept napping *while* working, on company time.

We can just hear the napaphobes reacting: "Now you've gone too far! That's ridiculous!" But have we? While napping can increase productivity after one awakens, we believe it also can improve productivity *while* one is napping. How else could we have written this book?

The productivity nap comes in many sizes

Naps at the workplace are called productivity naps. In *The Art of Napping,* we talked about three types of naps: the *preventive* nap, the *preparatory* nap, and the *pleasurable* nap. Taken at the work site, any of these would be considered a productivity nap.

The *preventive* nap prevents sleep deprivation, headaches, ill health, and other maladies. When taken at the work site, its purpose is to avoid losses in productivity due to lack of sleep. Preventive naps taken in the mid-day help avoid that afternoon dip in performance and mood. Night workers often take them in the early morning hours.

The *preparatory* nap helps workers function better when they must stay awake for long periods of time. When workers are working long hours to meet deadlines and extraordinary production standards, a preparatory nap allows them to be productive during the later hours of an extended workday.

The *pleasurable* nap is designed for those who nap just because they like it! During break time, workers engage in activities they like: eating, exercising, etc. Napping for some people is just as pleasurable

Workplace napping has fostered other napping types. In addition to the three types one can take at the break, there are naps that impact productivity during the nap itself. We call these productivity naps the *problem solving* nap and the *procrastination* nap. These two new types of naps help to define what is meant by napping while you work.

A napping brain is a working brain

During the first few minutes of our nap we are in a very light sleep, somewhat aware of our environment. We may feel only "half-asleep." We can "listen" to a presentation and nap at the same time. How many of us have steadfastly maintained that we were in fact listening when someone observed us napping? It's just that during the early minutes of our nap nothing important was going on so we didn't have to respond.

Up until 20–30 minutes, we're still in a lighter sleep relative to the deep sleep that occurs 40 minutes to an hour after falling asleep. While we may not be learning new information during a nap, we may be reorganizing information we already have. Creativity is often a matter of seeing new connections between old things. That is why people solve problems while napping.

The problem solving nap just happens—sometimes when we least expect it. We awaken with a different perspective on how to approach a problem. We thought we were taking a preventive, preparatory, or pleasurable nap and upon awakening find that it was a problem solving nap. What a napping bonus! The budget is clearer, the plan takes shape, the files are easier to organize, a new direction suggests itself, and/or we now know what to say. Then you know that a problem solving nap just happened.

A napping brain can also be a procrastinating brain

We were first alerted to this type of productivity nap by a caller to a radio talk show. We were discussing productivity naps, and she mentioned that sometimes she naps before taking a course of action. What differentiates this nap from the problem solving nap is that upon awakening the problem has taken care of itself and needs no action on her part. She calls it the procrastination nap. We took a long time and many naps before deciding to also call this nap the procrastination nap. And the more we procrastinated, the better we liked the name.

Any company or person can profit from the procrastination nap. Upon reflection, we realized that we first learned this nap as toddlers. Our parents would often send us napping when we were about to do something stupid—like bite a sibling or destroy furniture: When we awoke from the nap, we were no longer interested in that particular stupid thing.

Likewise, the workplace often confronts us with an interpersonal issue or job task that we think needs action right away. Taking action immediately seems as important now as biting our sister (brother) or destroying the furniture did then. But before we do something that may feel good in the moment, but in retrospect might be stupid for the long term, we might try a procrastination nap—and then see if it still makes sense. Sometimes what we don't do is as important as what we do, and the procrastination nap can sometimes do the hard work of separating the wheat from the chaff—while napping.

A napping gender gap?

Admit it. Some of you think napping is primarily a male activity. While some women are known to be expert at it (like Camille), it seems that most women don't practice the art of napping, or at least rarely brag about it like men do. In support of this theory, we received numerous comments from women about their father's napping exploits, but rarely about their mother's. Other sources seemed to confirm a napping gender gap.

An Internet article stated, "If you are male and the other side of 20, taking a few winks after working, eating, or just thinking hard is really important. . . . Women (especially wives) will never understand the joys of napping."

The Workplace Napping Survey discounts the notion of a napping gender gap. Women are approaching or surpassing men in many things these days, and napping appears to be another.

Forty-five percent of our current respondents who nap at work are women. We suspect several reasons for this unexpectedly high percentage:

- Women who become mothers are staying in the work force. According to the National Sleep Foundation, 51% of pregnant or recently pregnant women take at least one weekday nap. Mothers who developed this habit during pregnancy are not giving it up when they return to work.

- Working women are still "doing it all." The Families and Work Institute reports that working women remain responsible for most home chores, such as cooking, cleaning, bill-paying, and shopping. Women survey respondents say that napping at work makes them more productive.

- Working women are going public about their napping. For example, Dorothy Granger is an insurance agent who napped at work for years. Dorothy would lie down on the floor behind her desk for a 20-minute productivity nap whenever she could. Her workplace napnomics were the floor and the privacy provided by the desk (or so she thought). Dorothy's office had interior windows and her desk faced them. When she would lie down, unbeknownst to her, her feet would extend beyond the end of the desk. One day a colleague burst into the office as he thought Dorothy had died. Dorothy, of course, was very much alive and living the good napping life.

- Women business leaders are playing a role in designing workplace napping spaces. Karen Gould is an interior designer at Gould, Evans & Goodman—an architectural, interior design, land use planning and graphics firm. The 165 employees work long hours, often very late and under deadline pressure. Karen believed that a nap spot should be made available to them for a 30-minute respite. She originally wanted a nap room, but all the rooms were needed as work space. So she decided to try movable, lightweight napping tents which could be positioned wherever room was available. The three one-person "Spent Tents," complete with alarm clocks, earphones, music, sleeping bags, inflatable air mattresses, and pillows, are often used around lunch time. The graphics department designed a moon and Zs that hang in the nap area from the ceiling and sayings that are hung on the wall. Karen says that to her knowledge employees have never abused the napping policy.

Eliminating the gender gap

A preponderance of non-workplace nappers who respond to our survey are women aged 20–35. When asked why they aren't napping at work, they say it's not because they don't want to nap to improve their productivity. For 53% of them the reason is fear of being fired or frowned upon. An additional 7% think that the nature of the work prevents napping.

- A 28-year-old auditor sent chills up our spines when she wrote, "My job is terribly exciting, and I couldn't imagine sleeping on the job and missing the excitement."

Another 18% don't nap at the workplace because of poor nap habits. Some women are simply not proud or confident enough about napping (effective napping habit #1)

- A 33-year-old architect dreamed: "I can't rest properly in public. Instead I wish the siesta would be introduced worldwide—so we could all take a decent break from 2–4 P.M., when everybody's in a coma anyway."

Ensuring a method for on-time awakening (effective habit #3) is a problem for some women:

- An apparently sleep-deprived advertising agency employee succinctly stated, "I would not wake up."

Overcoming sleep inertia (effective habit #6) is a problem for other women:

- An administrative assistant, age 22, said: "I work in a doctor's office, so I could sneak into a room; but by the time I fell asleep, it would be time to wake up and I would feel more tired."

THE ART OF NAPPING AT WORK

Small percentages of these women seem to lack napping creativity and initiative: 5% say they don't nap because nobody else does; another 5% choose not to answer, and 12% say there is no good place to nap at work.

As napping policies change and prideful, effective, creative napping behavior emerges, the next century of women will erase completely the napping gender gap.

Napping across the ages

Is there a napping age gap? How many people picture the napper as an older male, disheveled and sprawled on a couch, with drool sliding out of his mouth? That's not the picture that respondents to the Workplace Napping Survey paint.

Contrary to some people's expectations, 48% of the survey respondents who are workplace nappers are age 35 and below, 42% are 36–54, and only 10% are above 55. Workplace napping clearly spans a worker's life.

Particularly encouraging is the number of young workers napping at work. These figures bring hope to the napping community. Napping, unlike youth, is not wasted on the young—it's perfected by the young. Young adulthood is the time to start a family, a career, and your napping life. At one time napping development was arrested when careers began, but that no longer appears to be the norm.

Employees are people, too

Some employers have the attitude that other parts of employees' lives aren't important. Data from the Families and Work Institute suggest that 75% of the work force feel "used up at the end of the workday" sometimes to very often. Some employers might be pleased with this figure and feel they've gotten their money's worth. Our guess is that employers with nap friendly policies would think differently.

Fully functioning organizations know that most workers do have a life outside the workplace. For "quality time" with family, friends, and community activities, the worker has to have some energy left after work. A worker's responsibility is to arrive at the workplace with the energy needed to do good work. Conversely, could it not be part of a organization's responsibility to have the worker leave work with energy to invest in the remainder of the day?

One of our most memorable interviews was with Adam Glogowski, an employee of Yarde Metals. In the presence of CEO Craig Yarde, Adam told us that not only does his noon nap make him a more productive worker, it makes him a better father and husband: He has something left when he goes home to his family and children.

Our case histories of various companies tell us that nap-friendly companies believe their firms' greatest assets are their employees, *and they treat them that way*. We were struck by how proud the company spokespersons are about their companies' benefits in many areas. When a company truly cares about their employees, the employees feel better about themselves and their company.

Nap friendly polices show that employers care—about their employees' health and safety. Nap friendly policies show that employers trust their employees—to do what's best for themselves and their companies. Nap friendly policies show that employers are interested in employees living complete lives outside the workplace. Nap friendly firms are 100% convinced that satisfied workers lead to satisfied customers.

To nap or not to nap? —It's no longer the question

As we go into the future, the question will be *when* and *where* to nap, not *whether* to nap. Circadian Technologies has already designed a corporate training program called Nap Power to educate workers on the effective use of napping. Before the sleepy-dust epidemic, we knew that sleep and food were important ingredients of life. In the 20th century, we focused on food but forgot about the essential nature of sleep. However, we're finally waking up to the life-enhancing value of sleep. An analysis of studies that looked at sleep, diet, and exercise concluded that healthy sleep is the most important factor in increasing longevity. In the 21st century, changes in the workplace can ensure that we overcome the virus destroying the quality of our work and our lives. The napping community will continue to open employers' eyes to the merits of napping:

THE FUTURE OF WORKPLACE NAPPING

- "I encourage you to promote workplace napping. If we do more napping, I won't have so many people at meetings with their eyes rolling around in their heads and their heads snapping back and forth."

Like the napping pilot, too many workers are on autopilot. The computer is on, the business is open, people are talking—but for certain periods of time no actual work is occurring. The sleepy-dust virus is in control.

One manager gave us a glimpse of the future when he wrote about his company's nap policy: "We don't have one yet. However, when we rewrite our policies and procedures concerning breaks, I will include napping as an acceptable way to use break time."

A worker who had read some of our material on napping said: "After reading it, I don't feel the least bit guilty about my napping habits. My God, I'm normal after all!"

z   z   z

We hope that after reading *The Art of Napping at Work,* you also see workplace napping as the no-cost, natural way to increase our work productivity and satisfaction.

Good Napping to You!

Bill and Camille

In response to popular demand, "napping guru" Bill Anthony continues his tradition of addressing a serious problem (sleep deprivation) in a humorous way that restores our sanity. In *The Art of Napping at*  *Work,* he and wife Camille take 1997's acclaimed sleeper, *The Art of Napping,* to the workplace.

See why and how so many smart business-people are laying down at the job: to enhance creativity, productivity, and the bottom line—PLUS have energy left for themselves and families at the end of the work day.

Praise for Bill Anthony and *The Art of Napping*

"*The Art of Napping* has changed me from a secret napper to an outgoing, up-front napper. . . . After reading Bill Anthony's book, I nap with confidence and pride in my expertise at doing it."

—**Andy Rooney,** Tribune Media Services

"Wake up and read this. Then you can nap." —*The Wall Street Journal*

"Anthony has become the nation's favorite wakeup call because sleep-deprived Americans are tired of being tired." —*Sacramento Bee*

"*The Art of Napping:* Tired? Overworked? Stressed out? Try this ancient, no-cost, no-sweat route to health and happiness." —*Yoga Journal*

"*The Art of Napping* is a great hit around the office. This little book covers everything from nap management to the great nappers of history."
—*Prevention* Magazine

"After reading *The Art of Napping*, Craig Yarde decided to integrate a nap room into the blueprints for his new corporate headquarters."
—*U.S. News & World Report*

"Napping on the job is nothing to yawn about." —*Toronto Star*

"A new American hero has emerged. He's Boston University professor William Anthony . . . " —**Bridgeport, Connecticut** *Valley Sentinel*

"The world's preeminent nap expert, Boston University's William Anthony . . ." —*Boston Business Journal*

"Anthony is a consummate napper." —*Associated Press*

"William Anthony is one professor who is likely to be understanding when students fall asleep during his lectures." —*The New York Times*

The Art of Napping, also published by Larson Publications, is available through National Book Network and most major distributors
(112 pages, 20 illustrations, $9.95 paperback)